Seeker To The Dead by A.M Burrage

Alfred McLelland Burrage was born in Hillingdon, Middlesex on 1st July, 1889. His father and uncle were both writers, primarily of boy's fiction, and by age 16 AM Burrage had joined them. The young man had ambitions to write for the adult market too. The money was better and so was his writing.

From 1890 to 1914, prior to the mainstream appeal of cinema and radio the printed word, mainly in magazines, was the foremost mass entertainment. AM Burrage quickly became a master of the market publishing his stories regularly across a number of publications.

By the start of the Great War Burrage was well established but in 1916 he was conscripted to fight on the Western Front. He continued to write during these years documenting his experiences in the classic book War is War by Ex-Private X.

For the remainder of his life Burrage was rarely printed in book form but continued to write and be published on a prodigious scale in magazines and newspapers. In this volume we concentrate on his supernatural stories which are, by common consent, some of the best ever written. Succinct yet full of character each reveals a twist and a flavour that is unsettling.....sometimes menacing....always disturbing.

There are many other volumes available in this series together with a number of audiobooks. All are available from iTunes, Amazon and other fine digital stores.

Index of Contents

CHAPTER I
TENDERHOOKS

The little girl in bright green had a special smile for Roger Moorlock when he called, or so he liked to think. She was pretty enough to seem interesting, and he was of an age and temperament to be interested.

"Oh, Mr. Moorlock?" she said, but by way of greeting rather than interrogation. "Mr. Soames is expecting you, I think he is disengaged. I'll go and see."

She jumped up from the chair before her typewriter, knocked on a great shining mahogany door, and opened it to stand for a moment -only under the lintel. Roger heard nothing, and she faced him again so quickly that he could hardly believe that she had exchanged a word or a look with anyone else.

"Will you go in, please?"

Roger smiled and went swiftly and quietly past her. The doorway was high, but instinctively he lowered his head to go through. Ever since he had achieved the height of six feet two inches he had suffered in unfamiliar doorways, and his sub-consciousness took charge whenever he made to enter a strange room.

Mr. Soames, who nodded from the far side of an impressive desk, was—when on his legs—nearly a foot shorter than his client. He was a little, smooth-shaven, bald-headed, pinch-faced man who looked rather like an unjovial monk; or he could have played in melodrama as the mean and rascally attorney with hardly any makeup. But his speech and manner were genial as became his business—which was to effect introductions between those who desired employment and those who wished to employ.

There was always a private tutor or two up Mr. Soames's sleeve, but his was not mainly a scholastic agency. His stock-in-trade—as he privately called it— consisted more of companions and secretaries with special qualifications. All manner of queer fish had come into Mr. Soames's net, but their queerness was no concern of his. He had pocketed his dues and asked no more questions than were exigent; but much unuttered speculation had traced the network of lines around his eyes.

"Oh," he said, "good morning. Sit down. I'm glad you managed to call early, because I wanted a word with you before I get you to call again a little later. I have—er—there is a Dr. Garrow who would like to meet you."

"Oh? *Doctor* Garrow?"

"He told me he was a doctor of science and medicine and—er—I think something «lse. I gather, from what he said, that he had studied at two or three Continental universities besides Cambridge. He became interested in you directly I told him that you had taken a First in Modern Languages, and then he picked on your name. Wanted to know if you were related to a certain Miles Moorlock who was with nim at Trinity."

"Miles Moorlock? Why, that would have been my grandfather!"

Mr. Shames smiled.

"He certainly doesn't look as old as that, but really he might be any age. A very peculiar man, I should say, and really I don't know how you would suit each other. But the main point—as it strikes me—is that he offers five hundred a year, and it's a residential post."
The younger man's eyebrows went up.

"Five hundred? What languages does he want?"

"He didn't say. He goes off at tangents. He asked one or two odd questions about your physique and what I imagined your temperament to be. I showed him copies of some of your references, but he seemed hardly to be interested. I think he is a man who will make up his mind when he has seen you. If you can make it convenient to come back at about a quarter past twelve—will you? I can then introduce you."

Roger Moorlock was smiling.

"Yes, rather, I'll come and meet him. And—suppose it comes off—where shall I have to go?"

"He lives at Dravington—in Berkshire."

"Good Lord!"

"Yes," said Mr. Soames, "—where that grave has been violated. Were you thinking of that?"
"That and—something else. I know some people there. Or rather I suppose they're still there. One of my best friends at school was the son of the parson. I met his father and mother and sister two or three times when they came down to the school. But Reggie—that's the son—is in the Army and I think he's out East now. Still, I shall be seeing his people. That's to say if—"
Mr. Soames cut him short.

"Do you mind," he asked quietly, "taking a hint from me?"

"Not in the least. Why?"

Mr. Soames hesitated. Mr. Soames looked down his nose. He wore a slightly strained expression, as if he were holding his breath while marshalling his thoughts.

"Mr. Moorlock," he said at last, "I am not a very imaginative man and I am only an amateur of psychology. Still, a great many strange people have passed in and out through that door, and not the least strange of them is Dr. Garrow. One gets—how shall I say?—impressions of people which cannot easily be translated into words. It would be useless to ask me the reason for what I am about to say, for I could not give it even if I wished. Bluntly—if you want that job I shouldn't tell him that you know the local parson."

Roger stared and then nodded very slowly.

"O-oh!" he murmured, and then raised his voice to its normal pitch. "Yes, but he's bound to find out."

A smile of ancient wisdom appeared on Mr. Soames's face.

"If I were you," he said, "I should let him find out afterwards. But you must please yourself about that. Anyhow I shall see you later."

The hint was so broad that Roger could not fail to see and take it.

"All right," he said with half a laugh, "I'll remember what you said. Good-bye for the present."

Roger went out briskly and turned right, to walk up into the Strand. Something more than the mere incline quenched his speed, and the hand thrust into a trouser pocket had something of the function of a minister of finance considering ways and means.

To be sure he knew already the total value of the coins embraced by his fingers. Crudely massed into shillings and pence they amounted to so little. Beyond them there were three pounds still in the Post Office Savings Bank. And beyond those three pounds there was nothing.

He had tried and abandoned—or meant to abandon— that dull means to a dead end which is called school- mastering. Two terms had been his limit anywhere, and always at inferior schools. Headmasters had envied him —privately and even openly—a better degree than their, own. The speech and manners of the boys had irritated him; and the irritation was twofold because in dark moments of introspection he had cursed himself for a snob. Modern Languages may suggest a winning trick in Commerce—until one considers the army of underlings and unemployed who have also acquired them. A Blue would have carried him over the heads of others into the upper circles of the schoolmastering trade; but he had narrowly missed two—for Boxing and Rugby Football—and misses do not count.

There was an A.B.C. tea-shop on the corner at the top of the street, and, since the smoking-room was closed, the ground-floor was well sprinkled with customers, even at that hour of the morning. Roger secured a table to himself, but not for long: for a fussy, dapper little man carrying an attache case came and sat' opposite.

The fussy, dapper little man ordered exactly what Roger thought he was going to order—a cup of tea and a scone and butter. And because he had fulfilled unspoken prophecy Roger began to take a furtive interest in him.

He was a sandy man, with sandy hair, a sandy moustache and a sandy complexion. Rimless glasses with a gold, or rolled gold attachment, clung to his nose» and behind them—possibly because they magnified— blue-grey eyes bulged prominently.

Almost unconsciously Roger began trying to sum him up. He was a worker in an office and a dweller in a suburb—doing amazingly well from his own point of view. Probably he bullied and was worshipped by a wife much larger than himself. He was a mine of information on a multitude of subjects beyond his concern. At the office, this know-all was disliked and respected by all—respected even by his chief whom, all unwittingly, he had contrived to bluff. Smith—surely his name was Smith—knew how many male orphans there 'were in Corsica, when dog-licences were first introduced into Denmark, and the ancient marriage superstitions once prevalent in the Isle of Cyprus. And of course he knew what Germany was going to do next and what Holland was going to do after that.

The attache case came open. It contained, among other things, sandwiches rosy with tomato juice. But these remained, and out came a copy of a daily newspaper. Mr. Smith had been reading it in the train, he was going to continue reading it now, and in the evening he would take it home so that his wife might save a penny and remain *au fail* with current events.
Mr. Smith read for only a minute or two. The glittering eye of the Ancient Mariner focussed the deputy of the Marriage Guest. Mr. Smith spoke.

"Very odd affair—that case down at Dravington," he said. "Do you know what I think?"

"I've only just glanced at the paper. I just saw something about a grave and a body. I suppose it's another poison case."

"Oh, no. The body wasn't exhumed. Not officially exhumed, I mean. It was stolen."

"How?"

"Grave dug open at night. Thurley had only been in it a week. Coffin and all stolen. Reminds you of those old tales of the body-snatchers. People, you know, used to dig up bodies and sell them to doctors so that they could get a bit of practice. You've read Stevenson? Well, do you know what I *think?"*

Roger smiled. There was something captivating in the urgent and omniscient manner.

"Well?" he said invitingly.

"Well, this Thurley was a brilliant scientist, and it was known that for years he had been studying up something or trying to invent something. But it doesn't say that anything important's been found among his papers. Now it looks to me as if he had his secret buried with him— or somebody thought he had. But what a thing to go and do! I mean to say—take a corpse out of a grave and pinch—I mean, steal it, coffin and all."

"It certainly seems a bit odd," Roger agreed.

"A bit odd! The whole thing's odd from beginning to end! What do you make of a man who keeps a gold poker in his dining-room?"

"A gold what?"

"Poker. Po-ker. For the fire, you know. After his death somebody noticed the colour and weight, and it turned out to be gold. Sounds- daft, doesn't it? But there! All brilliantly clever men are a bit funny in the head. Well, one or two people have said that I'm not all there. But only in fun, of course. Now you mark my words. It's almost bound to come out sooner or later. The man or-men who exhumed that body thought there were some valuable papers buried with it."

"Then why didn't they search the coffin in the graveyard and leave it there?"

There was a slight pause. Mr. Smith, cornered, yet declined to be nettled. Into a manner tremendously profound he wove a thread of intellectual coquetry.

"Ah," he said, "that's where you've got to do a bit of *thinking.* I've done my thinking already; and I'll tell you what."

"What?" Roger echoed.
Mr. Smith became confidential and enormously impressive. The right—or Ancient Mariner—eye glittered and bulged behind its magnifying pane.

"If I should happen to meet you again after all this is cleared up—if it ever is cleared up—"

"Yes?"

Mr. Smith's tone became less confidential than triumphant.

"—I'll ten to one be able to tell you that—what—I'm —thinking—now—is—dead—*right*!"

CHAPTER II
DR. GARROW

Garrow was not a large man, but his personality filled the room. His face—or rather the colour of it—was extraordinary. It was something more than a healthy red or pink. Pink it was, and pink the same shade all over, with the vivid pinkness of a chocolate filling. In deep contrast was his white hair, and of this there was great profusion. He looked as if he had not lost a hair since he was twenty. He wore it brushed straight back, and it shone with something of the glow of a snowfield in winter sunshine.

For a moment he wondered of what the face with its crown of hair reminded him; and then it came to him. "Raspberries and cream," he thought; and bit his lip upon inopportune laughter. And indeed Dr. Garrow was no figure of fun. His personality radiated something awe-inspiring. There are many sorts of awe, alike in that they spring from power—power unknown or power made manifest.

"Oh, Dr. Garrow"—Mr. Soames was speaking—"this is Mr. Moorlock, of whom I have been speaking. Mr. Moorlock—Dr. Garrow."

Dr. Garrow rose and bowed from the shoulders in the Continental fashion.

"How do you do?" he said, in a rich, mellow voice which somehow matched his raspberries-and-cream appearance. "I have been hearing about you and I should like a little chat with you. Perhaps Mr. Soames has another room where we could talk privately for a minute or two."
Mr. Soames rose at once.

"You can talk here," he said. "I want to examine some files in the next room. You will be quite undisturbed." He hurried out, leaving them alone together; and Dr. Garrow uttered a peculiar chirruping sound—a habit of his, as Roger was soon to discover—and looked the young man up and down.

"You were at Cambridge, I understand?"

"Yes, sir. I have just learned that you knew my late grandfather."

"Oh," laughed Dr. Garrow with another chirrup, "I met him many years after he'd gone down. I hope you hadn't the impression that I was up in his year. That would make me a very old man indeed."

As Dr. Garrow spoke Roger was wondering how old he really was. He was so strangely ageless that Roger would have been surprised at whatever he might be told'. Garrow went on speaking.

"You're a big man, Mr. Moorlock. Were you good at games? Are you good at games, I mean? I can't stand weaklings. Come here, if you don't mind, and let me feel your arm."

Roger, mystified, smiled and presented his right biceps. Dr. Garrow attempted to dig his fingers into it and nodded, apparently satisfied.

A piece of luck fell to Roger a few minutes later. Mr. Smith, having nourished his mighty brain, rose and went; and with that absence of mind which is considered part and parcel of genius, he left behind him his morning paper—thereby depriving Mrs. Smith of her daily dip into the news.

Roger watched him go and basely refrained from reminding him. He was in that condition when even pennies must be weighed, and while it appeared as if the worst of his troubles might soon be over he had learned by hard experience the folly of counting unhatched chickens. He had told Mr. Soames the literal truth in saying that he had only just glanced at the paper. He had glanced at the back of somebody else's. *"Sacrilege at Dravington"* had caught his eye; and the name Dravington had reminded him at once of Reggie Vallence and his people.

Directly he began to read the name Vallence sprang to- his gaze. "In an interview the Vicar, the Rev. T. W. Vallence said: 'I cannot imagine who would have committed this ghastly desecration, nor why. The Vicarage stands some two hundred and fifty yards from the churchyard, and we should have been very unlikely to hear any sounds made by the desecrators.

" 'Such, a case is fortunately unique in my experience. I did not know the deceased at all well. He was somewhat o, a valetudinarian. I know him to be the author of many inventions, his latest, I believe, being an improved instrument for testing the blood- pressure.

" 'I cannot imagine the reason for this ghastly crime. Any papers of value which he may have left behind would of necessity be in the hands of his executors. I have heard rumours that he possessed some secret with which he intended to die; but even if that were true the secret would surely be recorded in his heart and never committed to writing"

"And that," thought Roger, "looks fair[4] enough. A pretty odd sort of bird the late lamented gentleman seems to have been. I wonder if the other odd bird knew him. Possibly not, since the late Mr. Thurley seems to have been a recluse. Dravington seems to have had some queer people in it."

Roger sat in the Temple Gardens until he thought it was time to call once more upon Mr. Soames. The girl in green with the special smile asked him to wait. Some body, it seemed, was already with Mr. Soames.

But Roger was hardly seated when the house telephone buzzed at the girl's elbow and she took down the receiver and listened for a moment or two to a voice speaking in the next room. She said, "Very good; I'll tell him"—and turned to Roger.

"Mr. Soames was asking if you'd come. He says, will you go in, please."

Roger knocked and entered and looked inquiringly at Mr. Soames—looked long and inquiringly, indeed, because he was fighting a temptation to turn and stare at the other occupant of the room. The quick glance he had given to Dr. Garrow received in turn an impression which seemed to remain, upon the eyes and burn under the lids.

"If you come to me it means your cutting yourself entirely from the rest of the world. From local society, I mean. Indeed, I doubt if people would want to have much to do with you. It is the way of fools—and English fools in particular—to suspect any man they are incapable of understanding. You will have no society but mine. The condition may seem hard to you; but that is why I am offering five hundred a year. Do you wish to accept it?"

"Yes," said Roger without hesitation.

"You must understand this—that anything unusual you may see, or fancy you see, in my house, is not to be mentioned outside. I must make that perfectly clear to you. I do not enjoy being discussed. I cannot think whom you would find to talk to, except the yokels; but if I discovered that you had spoken to anybody outside concerning my affairs I should—I should be greatly displeased, Mr. Moorlock."

Roger started as if he had been touched by a needle. Never until then could he have imagined such a dreadful intensity put into such mild words. He looked up, his nerves tingling with a kind of shock.

And he looked into a shining pink face smiling serenely. Dr. Garrow was looking as sweet and as mild as the boy in the famous picture which is called *"Bubbles."*

"So," he proceeded, "what do you say?"

Roger's mind was already made up. Certainly he would put up with this monstrosity for a time—while he was saving something out of ten pounds a week.

"I believe you would find me discreet enough," he said, "and I accept the conditions."

There was a pause and Roger's lips had parted to speak again.

"Yes?" said Dr. Garrow.

"I beg your pardon," said Roger, "I didn't speak."

It was true, for he had checked himself in time. Clearly this was not the occasion tc let Dr. Garrow know that he knew the people at the Vicarage. But the thought, coming unbidden, refused io expand. It was useless for him to ask himself why he thought that Dr. Garrow might not like the clergy nor the clergy like Dr. Garrow. When he had proved how invaluable he was he could allow the truth to be known.

Dr. Garrow's return to geniality was announced by another chirrup.

"And now," he said, "—now that everything is so far arranged—when can you come? Would the day after tomorrow be too soon for you?"

"No."

"Now tell me," he said, "what you did at Cambridge."

"I took a First in Modern Languages—"

"Yes, yes, so I have heard. But what games did you play? Did you get your Blue for anything?"

"No. I played two or three times in the fifteen but I didn't get my Blue. And at boxing—"

"Ah!"

"I got into the heavy-weight finals. But there was a man at Clare who could just beat me. He boxed against Oxford and against the Hospitals."

"Well, that's not so bad. Let me look at your face. Courage, now. I like courage. Indeed, it would be an essential if— Ah, plenty of it there, I think. I am enough of a psychologist to see that. So you think you might be useful to me, do you?

"My languages," said Roger, in a hurry to present his qualifications while the time seemed favourable—"I am pretty fluent in French, German and Spanish. I know no Russian nor modern Greek, but I have a smattering of Dutch, Portuguese and Danish."

"Yes," said Dr. Garrow indifferently, "I have some foreign correspondence sometimes and I am a poor linguist. You have strength and, I assume, courage. Are you faithful to those to whom you sell your sword?"

Roger laughed.

"I am afraid, Dr. Garrow," he said, "that I haven't one to sell."

Dr. Garrow smiled in turn.

"I think you know what I mean. If you took service with me you would stand by me, no matter what the occasion. You would neither betray me nor forsake me?"

Roger was puzzled and vaguely troubled.

"Of course not," he said with an uneasy laugh.

There was a pause.

"Listen," said Dr. Garrow suddenly, "I am in some respects a somewhat peculiar man. My studies revolve around a subject which—well, I should have to know you a great deal better before I told you. I dislike being talked about. For that reason my one servant—a host in himself—is deaf and dumb.

"Very well. May I expect you at about tea-time? There is one good afternoon train from Paddington—the three something. You had better look it up in the A.B.C. Here is my card with the address. I live about two miles from the station. And now I must wish you good morning. I come to town so seldom that, when I *do* come, I find that I have a great deal to do. Oh, by the way, I can't send to the station to meet you. I do not keep a car. But any of the porters will be able to tell you where to get a conveyance. Goodbye."

A minute or two later Roger found himself outside in the street. The smile on his face was thoughtful, but on the whole satisfaction outweighed misgiving. With at least a little of the immediate future secure he could invite his appetite to the kind of lunch of which it had been stinted for a long and hungry while. Food possessed his thoughts until his appetite was, to some extent, appeased and it was not until he had eaten half a large steak that two thoughts occurred to him.

"He didn't even mention that stolen body—and that's rather funny."

Certainly it was strange, seeing that he came from the same village; and here was a mystery which had already taken a hold on the popular imagination. Sharp upon this reflection came another.

"And he didn't give me any idea of the kind of work he wanted me to do—and that's funnier still."

CHAPTER III
VAGUE WARNING

Roger, on his return to the bed-sitting-room which had been his only abode for some while past, spent the better part of half an hour in considering the turn of events and then wrote a hasty letter to the Rev. T. Wilfred Vallence at the Vicarage, Dravington. It broke the ice of a few years, by asking after the welfare and progress of Reggie and begging to be remembered to Mrs. and Miss Vallence, and went on to announce his prospective arrival in the neighbourhood.

The letter was Well-disguised bait. He asked for no information concerning Dr. Garrow, but he was reasonably sure of receiving some—if only in the form of a hint—by return of post. But he had not to wait for even so long as that. At a quarter to eleven on the following morning, when he was smoking a pipe and thinking of going for a walk, his landlady tapped at the door and said:

"There's a gentleman to see you, Sir. Mr. Val Somebody he told me."

"Great Scott!" Roger guessed at once and, hearing a movement outside his door, he raised his voice: "Is that, you, Mr. Vallence? Come in."

The Rev. Vallence came in beaming, with extended hand. The landlady vanished behind his broad back. Roger took the hand.

"What a coincidence!" he exclaimed. "I'd just written to you? I didn't know you were in town. You'll find my letter waiting for you when you get home." Vallence's smile had faded.

"Oh, no, I shan't," he said quietly. "I've got it in my pocket. It came by the first post; and as soon as I could leave I got into Reading and caught a good train. Only took me three-quarters of an hour from there to Paddington."

Roger seemed a little dense.

"Then you know about my job?" he said. "Are you staying the night in town? Because, as I said in my letter, I'm going down there tomorrow and we might travel together. How are Mrs. Vallence and Miss Vallence? *And* Reggie? I wish he'd write more often. I haven't heard from him for—"

Vallence interrupted with a movement of the lips and uplifted hand. Then he sat in the chair which Roger was placing for him. He was a stoutish man with greying hair, red cheeks and kindly brown eyes. There was trouble in those eyes, turned now paternally on Roger.

"My dear boy," he said "—excuse me—you are only Reggie's age. I have made the journey specially to see you. There are certain things which it is best not to write. You understand me, I think. Besides, although I haven't a persuasive tongue it generally serves me better than my pen. I've come specially to see you—to beg of you to keep yourself out of that man's clutches."

"What man? Garrow?"

"Yes."

There was a spell of silence. Then Roger uttered a short, troubled laugh.

"Thank you," he said, "—thank you very much—for warning me and taking all this trouble. Do you mind— er—telling me what's wrong with him?"

"I wish to God I knew."

Roger sat still, a questioning smile on his face. After a while, Vallence continued: "I know what you are going to say, or at least think. I of all men have no right to prejudge my fellows. I have nothing definite against the man, no accusation which I could substantiate. But—I am by no means the only person who is sensitive with regard to "him. If I am wrong in saying it, then may I be forgiven. But—I say it. That man is Evil."

Roger inclined his head.

"Do you know—anything—" he began.

"My dear boy, I just know this—that that man is on the Other Side. Do you know what I mean by that? I'm not speaking as a parson, but just as an ordinary and, I hope, decent man."
Roger nodded.

"Yes, I think I know what you mean. But I don't see how it need affect me. His private life is his own business. If some time in the future we had a Postmaster General who was caught living in sin with the head wardress at Pentonville, I shouldn't expect all the Police and the Post Office people to come out on strike." Vallence laughed, but only for a moment.

"That is quite different. I think you know quite well what I mean. I have a very strong instinct about Dr. Garrow. There are those who do wrong things and are sorry; and there are others who do wrong and persuade themselves that there is no Infinite Being to offend. But that man knows. And he is on the Other Side—not as a blind dupe, but as an ally. Ever read Macbeth?"

"Yes."

"Then you know—'By the pricking of my thumbs, Something evil this way comes, Well, one needn't always be a witch to feel that."

Roger laughed.

"I know what you mean. Well, I didn't like the man myself. But—I don't see what harm he can do me."

"Don't find out too late."

A sudden thought struck Roger.

"You don't think he had anything to do with exhuming and stealing the body of that man Thurley?"

Vallence started slightly.

"I don't see why he should. I have no right to—"

He paused and looked aside, to resume in another tone:

"Now *that* was a most extraordinary and damnable business. Extraordinary and damnable!"
"I suppose you've no theory concerning who did it— and why?"

The Rev. Vallence began slowly to load a pipe.

"I think I know why. The late Mr. Thurley was a very brilliant man. He was an inventor, you know. I knew him fairly well. He did not come to church, but he allowed me to minister to him when he was dying. And he told me—as I suppose he must have told others— that he had a secret which would be buried with him. I think he meant buried *in* him—buried in his own heart. But no doubt somebody must have taken him more literally. He was a very strange man, quite a recluse like the other; but not an evil man. Indeed, he told me that his secret would not be for the good of mankind, and so he intended taking it with him."

Roger nodded once or twice.

"Excuse me for asking," he said. "Perhaps I oughtn't to. You haven't any idea of the nature of his secret?"

"None at all. And perhaps it amounted to nothing. I am not slandering the man in saying that he was undoubtedly mad. A mad genius, no doubt, but the madness was there. And once a man is subject to delusions,, one can never tell. He thought he had some secret which would revolutionize the world—he told me as much—and for the world's sake he meant to keep it. Nothing was buried with him. The undertaker and his men can swear to that. So those who committed the sacrilege did their crime and took their pains for nothing."

"Yes, but Mr. Vallence, here's the odd thing. Where *is* the body? One hears and reads that a human body is almost impossible to conceal for any length of time." The Vicar shrugged his shoulders.

"Oh, no doubt it will come to light eventually. The ghastly thing has only just happened. And it happened so close to where I lay asleep at the time. If the wind had only been in the other direction I might have wakened and heard the ghouls at work. But none of us heard anything. The Police, of course, have been very active. The county detective—or whatever they call him —spent about two hours with me yesterday."

"Ah!" Roger smiled as he put a hopeless question. "I suppose he didn't tell you what he thought about it?"

The Rev. Vallence smiled faintly as he answered:

"No. He looked very wise, but he seemed fogged. I gathered from him that if he could discover a motive for the crime he could soon lay hands on those who did it. Alternatively, if he could find them first he would soon discover the motive."

Roger caught the faint gleam in his eye and laughed. "That's like the Police, I suppose," he said, "but I don't think they miss much. After all, there are very few unsolved mysteries nowadays.
And those the Police haven't cleared up—well, I think they've got a pretty good idea of the identity of the guilty party but they're just short of some little link of evidence."

"And occasionally too," said the Vicar dryly—"well, there is such a thing as public policy, you know. And now, look here, my dear fellow. Are you really going to the dev. . . . ahem!—that man?"

When Roger woke on the following morning—the day of his departure for Dravington—it was as if the sun of a bright day had dissolved his previous vague misgivings. Over night these had crowded upon him, exaggerated and distorted. The truth was, as he knew, that he was run down, and that his well-developed body had begun to feel the effects of weeks of stinting.

He treated it that morning to a good breakfast and searched his paper for further news of the strange affair at Dravington. But the "Stolen Body Mystery" was relegated to one' short paragraph under that heading. This meant—as indeed it was stated in other words— that there was no further news.

In mellow sunlight, and with his appetite thoroughly satisfied, he began to smile at his previous misgivings. At the same time he could excuse himself for having entertained them. Dr. Garrow was queer enough; and then of course that visit from Reggie Vallence's father was disturbing.

It served to prove to him that a man has but to look a little out of the ordinary and lead a secluded life to set all sorts of tongues wagging—even educated and charitable tongues. And once disturbing thoughts arise they grow and multiply, unless destroyed .like rats in a granary.

Why on earth, he wondered, had he suspected Dr. Garrow of having anything to do with the disappearance of that body? For the thought had been with him all the while. What on earth would Garrow, or anybody else, want with the dead body of an old dreamer who had babbled of a secret which he never meant to divulge? That cold clay in the coffin could tell him nothing. No, ignorance was written large over that ghastly incident, and ignorance was no disability of Dr. Garrow's.

Roger rose, humming to himself, and turned his thoughts elsewhere. He wondered—as he had often wondered—what Marjory Vallence was like to-day. "Nice kid," he had always thought, but then he had been prejudiced by his liking for her brother. "But not a bit pretty," he had to own. "A bit too like poor old Reggie." And at school poor old Reggie had been nicknamed Ears —for two reasons which were extremely prominent.

During the morning Roger packed the scanty contents of his wardrobe and the remainder of his personal possessions. When this was done he found that the old trunk, which once had reminded him of an adage about a quart and a pint pot, was obviously capable of holding a great deal more. It was some while since worn-out garments had been replaced, and the easy fastening of the lid was a tacit reminder that Dr. Garrow's offer had come at an opportune time. Nor, by an easy corollary, ought he to look elsewhere for some while to come unless—for some reason or reasons yet to be discovered—he found life with Dr. Garrow altogether intolerable.

There was a station at Dravington, on a branch line from Reading; but the trains were slow and infrequent, so that the lesser part of the journey took longer than the greater. Roger was the only passenger to alight from the afternoon train. He waited in sunlight to see his trunk pitched out, then he went to the door leading to the little booking hall, where a porter held out his hand for the ticket.

Roger laughed.

"I'm afraid so. I'm broke. But I shan't stay with him long if I don't like him. At the most I want to save thirty or forty pounds. That'll keep me going while I look for something else."

There was another pause. Vallence leaned forward a little and dropped his voice.

"I don't want to advise you to do anything underhanded," he said, "but I shouldn't go out of your way to tell him that you know—us!"

"Ah, I had a hint from the agent about that."

"Yes, he hates the clergy. I told you he was on the Other Side. Come and see us whenever you like, but— I'm afraid you'll be risking your job. Whether you tell him or not, he'll know. I tell you, that man's a devil and he knows nearly everything. You ought to hear some of the stories current about him—and they can't all be lies. No smoke without fire, you know. And look here, my dear boy, if you're in trouble—danger—"

"Danger"

"I don't know. I tell you I'm uneasy. If you want friends you know where to find them. For dear old Reggie's sake. Look here—if you're not well, or anything—I mean, if you can't get out for a day or two at a time, so that we can see you—just drop me a line. He wouldn't willingly admit me to his house, or rather that deaf mute of his would try to keep me out, but I'd see you somehow. Hullo, you're grinning. Laugh, if you want to, my dear fellow. Well—what?"
Roger's face slipped again.

"I'm awfully sorry. All this is awfully decent of you. But—you're making me feel like the nursery governess in one of those creepy, old-fashioned novels. You know^ —she had to go and look after the children of a homicidal bigamist in a haunted grange. And what that poor girl went through—for about twenty pounds a year—before she got all the hidden corpses decently interred and married the neighbouring squire's eldest son—" Vallence's face reddened and his lips parted. He shook with sudden laughter, turned his head for a moment and looked back with his face growing solemn again under its former cloud.

"I couldn't help it—but it's no laughing matter. Well, if you must go to him, I suppose you must. But don't forget what I told you about—should you need friends. And don't forget—don't forget that he's—on the *Other Side*!"

CHAPTER IV
MARJORY VALLENCE

When Roger woke on the following morning—the day of his departure for Dravington—it was as if the sun of a bright day had dissolved his previous vague misgivings. Over night these had crowded upon him, exaggerated and distorted. The truth was, as he knew, that he was run down, and that his well-developed body had begun to feel the effects of weeks of stinting.
He treated it that morning to a good breakfast and searched his paper for further news of the strange affair at Dravington. But the "Stolen Body Mystery" was relegated to one' short paragraph under that heading. This meant—as indeed it was stated in other words— that there was no further news.

In mellow sunlight, and with his appetite thoroughly satisfied, he began to smile at his previous misgivings. At the same time he could excuse himself for having entertained them. Dr. Garrow was queer enough; and then of course that visit from Reggie Vallence's father was disturbing.
It served to prove to him that a man has but to look a little out of the ordinary and lead a secluded life to set all sorts of tongues wagging—even educated and charitable tongues. And once disturbing thoughts arise they grow and multiply, unless destroyed .like rats in a granary.
Why on earth, he wondered, had he suspected Dr. Garrow of having anything to do with the disappearance of that body? For the thought had been with him all the while. What on earth would Garrow, or anybody else, want with the dead body of an old dreamer who had babbled of a secret which he never meant to divulge? That cold clay in the coffin could tell him nothing. No, ignorance was written large over that ghastly incident, and ignorance was no disability of Dr. Garrow's.

Roger rose, humming to himself, and turned his thoughts elsewhere. He wondered—as he had often wondered—what Marjory Vallence was like to-day. "Nice kid," he had always thought, but then he had been prejudiced by his liking for her brother. "But not a bit pretty," he had to own. "A bit too like poor old Reggie." And at school poor old Reggie had been nicknamed Ears —for two reasons which were extremely prominent.

During the morning Roger packed the scanty contents of his wardrobe and the remainder of his personal possessions. When this was done he found that the old trunk, which once had reminded him of an adage about a quart and a pint pot, was obviously capable of holding a great deal more. It was some while since worn-out garments had been replaced, and the easy fastening of the lid was a tacit reminder that Dr. Garrow's offer had come at an opportune time. Nor, by an easy corollary, ought he to look elsewhere for some while to come unless—for some reason or reasons yet to be discovered—he found life with Dr. Garrow altogether intolerable.

There was a station at Dravington, on a branch line from Reading; but the trains were slow and infrequent, so that the lesser part of the journey took longer than the greater. Roger was the only passenger to alight from the afternoon train. He waited in sunlight to see his trunk pitched out, then he went to the door leading to the little booking hall, where a porter held out his hand for the ticket.

Roger laughed.

"I'm afraid so. I'm broke. But I shan't stay with him long if I don't like him. At the most I want to save thirty or forty pounds. That'll keep me going while I look for something else."

There was another pause. Vallence leaned forward a little and dropped his voice.

"I don't want to advise you to do anything underhanded," he said, "but I shouldn't go out of your way to tell him that you know—us!"

"Ah, I had a hint from the agent about that."

"Yes, he hates the clergy. I told you he was on the Other Side. Come and see us whenever you like, but— I'm afraid you'll be risking your job. Whether you tell him or not, he'll know. I tell you, that man's a devil and he knows nearly everything. You ought to hear some of the stories current about him—and they can't all be lies. No smoke without fire, you know. And look here, my dear boy, if you're in trouble—danger—"

"Danger"

"I don't know. I tell you I'm uneasy. If you want friends you know where to find them. For dear old Reggie's sake. Look here—if you're not well, or anything—I mean, if you can't get out for a day or two at a time, so that we can see you—just drop me a line. He wouldn't willingly admit me to his house, or rather that deaf mute of his would try to keep me out, but I'd see you somehow. Hullo, you're grinning. Laugh, if you want to, my dear fellow. Well—what?"
Roger's face slipped again.

"I'm awfully sorry. All this is awfully decent of you. But—you're making me feel like the nursery governess in one of those creepy, old-fashioned novels. You know^ —she had to go and look after the children of a homicidal bigamist in a haunted grange. And what that poor girl went through—for about twenty pounds a year—before she got all the hidden corpses decently interred and married the neighbouring squire's eldest son—" Vallence's face reddened and his lips parted. He shook with sudden laughter, turned his head for a moment and looked back with his face growing solemn again under its former cloud.

"I couldn't help it—but it's no laughing matter. Well, if you must go to him, I suppose you must. But don't forget what I told you about—should you need friends. And don't forget—don't forget that he's—on the *Other Side*!"

CHAPTER IV
MARJORY VALLENCE

"Can I get a car or a cab or anything here?" he asked. "There's a taxi at the 'Bell,' sir, but it's just gone out. Saw it go over the crossing a few minutes ago."

Roger considered for a moment.

"You can send that trunk up for me?" he suggested. "Yes, sir. Carrier will be here any time now. Where too, sir?"

"Cattering House."

"You don't mean Dr. Garrow's place, sir?"

It seemed to Roger that the porter exhibited at least a mild surprise, and he answered abruptly: "Yes. Why?"

"Oh, nothing, sir. What I mean is—you'll be there when it comes? You see, sir, it's like this. If you and the Doctor was to go out together, it mightn't get left. I mean to say—his servant, being deaf and dumb—he sometimes don't hear—*feel,* I should say—the reverberations of the bell. And Hobbs won't just leave it on the step—not unless there's somebody there to sign."

"Oh, that'll be all right/' said Roger easily. "I'll tell Dr. Garrow. If you'll—"

He was interrupted. A moment before he had heard a light step inside the booking-hall. Now he heard his own name called.

"Mr. Moorlock—isn't it?"

Roger looked up sharply. The fair-haired girl with the dark blue eyes advancing towards him through the shade of the booking-hall seemed at first a complete stranger. But almost on the instant a family likeness sprang upon his consciousness. A slow smile came to his lips as he lifted his hat.

"It isn't Marjory?" he said.

He left the porter at once and went to her.

"Wouldn't you have known me?" she laughed. "I think I should have known you."

"Ah, but I was always older," he said, taking her hand. "It's awfully nice to see you again."

In slight bewilderment he stared at her, not intrusively but with the freedom of an old friend. For there was something analogous to friendship between them, although they had met but once and that occasion was some years since. Her brother Reggie was the link. Through Reggie they had heard a very great deal about each other.

"Your father came to see me yesterday," he said, and went off at a tangent. "I say!"

"Yes?"

"Nothing," he laughed. "I mean—I'm sure I shouldn't have known you."

"Freckles all gone now," she laughed. "And—look." She pushed back a curl with her little finger.
"D'you see?" she asked laughing. "Everybody thought I was going to have great, sticking-out ears like Reggie. I used to cry when I thought of Reggie's ears. But suddenly they stopped growing with the rest of me. Wasn't it a mercy?"

Roger uttered a non-committal grunt.

"Well, it's awfully nice to see you," he said hastily, "and what an odd thing that you should be on the station!"

"What! When I came to meet you?"

He smiled, politely incredulous.

"Let's go out," she resumed quickly, "and start walking. "I've got something to give you—er—Roger. You once told a small girl with freckles and Reggie-like ears that she could call you Roger, so I suppose she still can. Anyhow you've just called me Marjory. I'll walk with you part of the way."

"Rather," he said. "It's awfully pleasant to think that I shall be near you and your people—at least, while I've got this job. You'll let me float round to the Vicarage sometimes, I hope, when the old boy lets me off the chain."

They were outside the station building now and in step together. She looked up at him, but she did not smile in answering.

"I think Father told you," she said simply. "In fact, I know he did. He told us exactly what took place between you. If you come to see us it may mean that Dr. Garrow will—r—"

"Sack me?" he asked, laughing. "Nonsense!"

"You don't know him—yet. Dr. Garrow he calls himself. Do you know his real name?"
He shook his head, expecting to be "caught." Yet the word when it came filled him with a cold surprise which tingled in his blood the moment after.

"Legion," she said. "Do you know what I mean?"

He started a little and looked down frowning on her upturned face.

"Ye-es," he said. "Yes. But what makes you say that?"

"You'll know—in time. He's kept himself to himself to hide something. But he can't hide it all- Mention anything holy within his hearing and catch the first quick look on his face before he has time to smoothe it away. My dear, think we're all mad, if you must, but you'll know better before long."

He noticed, without smiling, the "my dear" which her intenseness had uttered and allowed her to ignore.

"And Trode," she continued, "is tarred with the same brush."

"Trode?"

"His creature. His deaf and dumb man. Nobody doubts why he keeps a deaf and dumb servant. But now everybody will wonder—as we're wondering—what he wants with *you*!"

"Well, I expect you know—I mean, I expect Reggie must have told you—that I'm rather useful at languages."

"Yes—and something else. Didn't you nearly get your Blue for something?"

"Nearly may be right," he laughed. "It means not quite. If you mean that I used to do a bit of boxing—"

"That's what I mean," said Marjory. "He's afraid of somebody—or something—and wants you to protect him."

Roger made no instant denial, for the same thought had been constantly in his own mind. "Yet if it were just that," he said, arguing against his own conviction, "he could get some East End pug, who scraps at the Blackfriars Ring whenever he can get put on, for—well, a good deal less than the salary he's giving to me.

She agreed, with a quick, mirthless laugh.

"Yes. But he wouldn't care about having such a man about him all the time. Besides, you've got references. And people would talk a great deal more—more even than they're talking now—if he chose that kind of man. It would simply advertise that he was scared of some-body or something. But nobody could wonder at a man high up in the Honours List getting a job with a man who at least pretends to be a scholar."

"No. It's all rather—er—uneasy. What do you think really is the matter with him?"

The girl eyed him askance.

"Father told you, I know," she said, after a slight hesitation. "He's on the Other Side."

"Do you mean a—er—a Satanist?"

"Yes, I think he's—possessed. Horses and dogs are terrified of him. So are children. Father thinks—I don't know if he told you—that he is a man who believes that Knowledge is Power. And he sought Forbidden Knowledge to obtain Forbidden Power."

Roger nodded; and then, in a sudden change of thought, he felt foolish and humiliated. He knew what he would have thought of such talk if he had heard it but a few days since; and here was he taking part in it. They were like a pair of mediaeval children, whispering together about the Witch. Suddenly he blamed in his mind the girl's father and the power of suggestion emanating, perhaps all unconsciously, from him. The Vicar disliked Dr. Garrow—with or without reason—and he had conveyed this dislike and distrust by telepathy more than by mere words.

"When shall I see you again?" he asked, with a sudden change of tone.

"Father doesn't think he'd like you to come to the Vicarage."

"Nonsense. I'm not the man's slave, nor going to be. I only want to hold my job until I've saved a few pounds. And besides I shan't tell him unless he asks." She laughed.

"You won't have to tell him. He'll know—without being told. He knows everything without being told. Ask any of the people around here. He knows you're talking to me now—"

"Oh, I say!" Roger protested, now really amused. "Very well! You won't laugh when you know him a little better. How long do you think you'll stay with him?"

"It depends on how long we can stick each other. With me it's the money, you see. I want to stay with him at least until I've got a few pounds behind me. For that reason I'm willing to put up with his whims—within limits."

The girl considered, frowning.

"Suppose he asks you not to go to the Vicarage—because he's had a row with Father? He could make any excuse. Don't just defy him and get the—er—bird."

"Well, but now I'm here I must see you sometimes, Marjory."

She laughed.

"I go to the post office every morning—or at least I'm generally out for something. Eleven o'clock-ish."

"Good! But suppose the slave is required at about that time? I haven't the least idea what I'm supposed to be going to do. But evidently my time isn't going to be my own."

"Well, if I don't see you then I' could make it three o'clock-ish in the afternoon. I'm generally free at that time and it's no distance from the Vicarage."

"Good! And where's the post office?"

"The shop you're looking straight at now, my poor blind boy, Jevons's."

"Thank you. And I suppose the church is underneath that spire over there?"

"How did you guess?" she laughed.

"And the Vicarage is somewhere near the church."

"You're getting like Dr. Garrow—positively uncanny."

"I've always been considered a fellow of unusual perception," Roger said, glad to feel that this not very sparkling banter was clearing the air a little.

"Then I suppose you've perceived that your road is opposite—up that hill. Further deduction will tell you that we have come to the parting of the ways. This is where you lift your hat and say, 'Good afternoon, Miss Vallence.' But before you do that—"

She paused and her manner changed back again. "Before you do that I've something to give you."

As she spoke she pushed into his hand a little parcel; brown paper tied over a cardboard box which was curiously heavy for its size.

"Oh, thanks very much," he said, taking it. "But what is it?"

"Something that I think you ought to have—in *that* house. But don't open it until you're in your room. You'll understand then. But see—you're Reggie's friend, aren't you?"

"And yours."

"Oh, that goes without saying—if you're Reggie's. Goodbye for the present, Roger. Take care of yourself."

"Same to you. And my kind regards to your father and mother. Oh, and tomorrow! Eleven-ish?"

"Or three-ish," she laughed. "Goodbye."

They parted. He stood looking after her for half a minute to see if she looked round. Then he crossed the road and took the branch road up the hill, the little parcel which he had just received from her lying heavy in his pocket.

CHAPTER V

STRAWS IN THE WIND

The gate by the empty lodge dragged on torn hinges and stood open just wide enough to give comfortable passage.

Roger, stepped over an arc of rut which the gate-end had scraped in the earth, and on to a drive lined by unclipped hollies. His feet sank in loose, heavy gravel, like sea-shore shingle, through which little spear-heads of grass protruded here and there.

Roger, on the look-out for anything from which an inference could be drawn, came at once to the conclusion that Dr. Garrow kept no outside staff. In order to keep up an appearance of at least semi-respectability in the sight of casual passers-by and thus avoid some of the risks of curiosity and intrusion, he had more gravel flung down whenever the weeds below made too much showing above the surface.

A minute later Roger found this surmise to be almost certainly correct. The gravel ceased when he had rounded a bend, and he followed a narrow track of grass, dandelions, daisies and stunted thistles, through which threaded two faintly defined footpaths.

The drive was tortuous all the way, and Roger smilingly divined the reason. Probably it had been made in the comically snobbish days of a century ago ' The hollies entirely concealed the house, and strangers who approached it might have a vastly exaggerated estimate of its surrounding acres.

However this may have been—for he never learned— the house, when he eventually reached it, proved to be a great deal older than the approach to it now led him to suppose. "1633," said the figures carved in oak above the open fire-place in the hall. t Roger, rounding the third or fourth curve, his mind preoccupied, received a sudden shock; for a step was | enough to bring him almost face to face with a stranger whose presence was hitherto unsuspected. With both of them treading the soft ground almost noiselessly the stranger too gave a start of surprise and guiltily thrust a hand into his breeches pocket. Roger heard the jingle of falling money.

The stranger wore a blue jersey under a worn blue coat. His complexion was only a shade less vivid than the hue of old Burgundy. He walked as if the weedy ground beneath his feet were a deck lifting and lurching at the will of the high seas.

He proclaimed his calling in his first words to Roger.

"Beg pardon, sir."

"Got a few coppers to help a sailor?"

"No," said Roger. "What was that I saw you stowing away?"

The sailor thrust a cap a little back from his perspiring brow and disclosed a lock of flaming red hair. He ignored the question and spoke rapidly.

"It's like this here. We paid off last Thursday, down Southampton. I lives up in Warwick, I do. My fambly, like. Well, I writes and says I'm comin' home. They're expectin' me, like. But there's a place near Southampton—close to the Forest—where they has pony races. Now it ain't fair to have pony races quite so near where sailor-men come ashore."

He paused and coughed.

"Well, I got a bit left. Arter the races, I mean. So I starts out on the road. And I writes my brother to telegraph me some dough Reading post office. You see, I ain't drawn all my pay, so he knows it's all right. But walkin's thirsty work and—anyhow, something's happened so as I'm not goin' on to Reading tonight."

Roger, tired of the rigmarole, dipped his hand into his pocket.

"You've got money already," he said, "but here's sixpence for you."

"Thank 'ee, sir. I see you goin' up to the big house. You don't belong there, do you, sir?"

Roger stared.

"Why?" he asked bluntly.

The sailor gave him an ingratiating smile.

"Well, sir, it's like this. I've just told you the gorspel truth. But it ain't the tale I pitched *'im.* Told 'im I 'adn't got a friend or a relation in the world. You see, sir, you bein' young and understanding-like, I could tell you just how things was. But 'im—no, that wouldn't do for *him.* Anybody could read that gent's character, sir."

The simplicity of the sailor in this last amazing statement blazed .upon Roger and shocked him into sudden laughter. The other grinned uncertainly, and as Roger made to pass on, lifted a finger to the peak of the cap which jutted above the vivid tuft of hair.

"Just a moment, sir. There ain't no need—is there?— to tell 'im that you've spoke to me and I've told you the truth. There's a reason for me asking."

The man's urgency was a mystery to Roger, but he answered good-humouredly.

"All right. I won't mention you. Good luck."

He passed on, little dreaming then of harm arising from this simple, small conspiracy. Sometime later his dreams were haunted by a ruddy face topped by a peak cap, and under the peak a thick wisp of hair like a tongue of flame.

Threading the tortuous avenue he came suddenly and unexpectedly to the end. The house came into sight like a picture suddenly unveiled, standing back in an open wilderness of untended gardens some eighty yards from the abrupt opening in the trees.

It was long, flat-fronted and, he supposed, Jacobean. Even at that distance the soft, mellow red bricks told their tale of age. But there were no Tudor gables nor dormer windows above the eaves to suggest the sixteenth century, and steps cut in a diminishing circle climbed to the main door between high, graceful pillars of a portico.

Even with the sun kindling and blazing on the glass between the stone mullions the house looked forbidding. "Oh, it must be haunted," Roger thought, intending to laugh; but he did not laugh. His mind had passed on into a maze of sinister conjectures. The environment of coarse grass and flowers struggling through the weeds of ruined beds took hold on his imagination and filled him with a sudden, cold dismay.

No wonder the old vicar saw—or imagined—something sinister in Dr. Gdrrow. What kind of man would live of his own free will in such an environment? It was not as if the ruined garden were an open and tacit confession of poverty. The man was going to pay his secretary ten pounds a week! Only a mind warped or perverted had allowed what Roger saw—the mind of a man who preferred the air of a vault to the wind on the heath, the bat's wing to the peacock's tail, the screech- owl's cry and the thunder cloud to the lark's song in open weather.

Roger, with a sinking of the heart, which he tried 'hard to keep at its normal level, mounted the steps and uttered a grim joke below his breath as he set a hand to the heavy, hanging bell-handle.

"H'm! Tried to give schoolmastering a miss. And now it seems I've come to another House of Usher. I bet this damned thing doesn't work."

But the bell responded, and even startlingly, to the tug he gave it. Somewhere in the servants' hall, behind closed doors and muffled by walls and distance he heard a single, heavy toll.

"Good Lord!" Roger was both aghast and amused. "He's got a church bell on the other end of this! If one were to pull the dap-med thing every half minute it would sound like a funeral."

There are occasions when the sinister and macabre may become laughable in their grotesquery. Roger had heard of a man who, having been given an opportunity to witness the Black Mass, had shocked the devotees of Satan by roaring with laughter. It was scarcely a gentlemanly requital to his sponsors, but Roger could well understand it.

Footfalls sounded within. The door of a lobby opened close at hand. Then a heavy bolt rattled and the door lurched open. Roger was prepared for anything—even for the tall, lean, moon-faced man in gleaming black velvet who spectacularly revealed himself.

So this was Trode, the deaf-mute.

Trode himself dispelled any doubt on that score by indicating his affliction with swift fore-finger movements to lips and ears. He then beckoned and stood aside, allowing Roger to pass him and walk through into the square inner hall, where he was faced by a broad stair-case which turned once at right angles in climbing to a railed gallery.

Here Roger drew a quick breath of surprise. He had expected dust and chaos to match the gardens without, but he trod highly polished boards on a floor fit for dancing.

The floor was strewn with skin rugs, and two suits of thirteenth century armour stood one on either side of the hearth. The dark oak panels of the wall opposite the fire-place were partly covered by a long tapestry. Above it were oil paintings hung haphazardly and wasted for being lost in shadow.

The tapestry, which Roger turned at once to examine, gave him immediately another disagreeable shock. It | was the work of mediaeval but not pious hands. A procession of folk and domestic animals—men, women and children, dogs, horses and cats—moved from right to left towards a black-hooded figure in the distance. Here art was made manifest in the vileness of all the faces. Even the horses leered, and on the faces of the dogs and cats were expressions half-human and voluptuous. The rearmost man of this vile procession had his back turned on the beholder. He was shown making a lewd gesture at the scraggy figure of a monk half way up a barren hillside—a monk who chided with one unlifted hand, and beckoned in vain with a hooked finger of the other.

As Roger stood gazing at this striking and rather appalling work of art he was aware of a soft footfall and a voice.

"Good afternoon, Mr. Moorlock—and welcome."

Dr. Garrow, pink, smiling and urbane had come, as it were, from the skies—a mellow sun to dispel shadows. It was strange and pleasant and quite surprising to find him, in these surroundings of his own choosing, an urbane man of the latter day world.

"I hope you travelled pleasantly," he continued, after Roger had responded; and suddenly and rather startlingly he stamped his foot.

Roger perceived the reason for this a moment later; for the deaf-mute, who had been about to pass out through the hall, halted and looked round. Dif. Garrow made quick gestures with his fingers; Trode responded with other and fewer gestures before hastily departing.

"He can read the lips fairly well," Dr. Garrow explained, "and of course he knows the ordinary deaf-and- dumb finger language. But, to avoid—ahem—eavesdropping we have our own code. He is, of course, completely deaf."

"Then how did he hear even that enormous bell just now?"

"He did not. He felt the reverberations. That explains the bell. He can—in a sense—'hear' it all over the house. Just as, a minute ago, he was aware of my stamping my foot. It is simpler and less fatiguing than giving him orders by concentrating my mind upon him. I can do that to an extent, but we are not perfectly en *rapport."*

Dr. Garrow paused calmly upon this somewhat startling utterance and then resumed.

"The conversation which you just now witnessed," he said, "merely concerned my ordering tea. Please sit down, and meanwhile take a cigarette. Oh, and by the way."

He paused and frowned.

"Have you brought with you into the house anything which—er—something in your pocket, I mean—which might offend a man of a certain temperament? My own temperament I mean, of course. I can't explain to you now. I shall not endeavour to do so until I know you better. But if you find you have brought with you something that a man with—er—certain views might not like, I must really ask you to get rid of it. It mustn't be here."

While he spoke he looked straight into Roger's face. His gaze encountered bland innocence. "Perhaps it is something hanging around your neck. A certain kind of—er—emblem. No? Well, I think you may guess when you come across it, and then you will know what to do. I am very susceptible to the presence of certain things, and something is causing me a great deal of discomfort. By the way, tea will not be here for about a quarter of an hour, and perhaps you would like to see your room and remove some of the invisible stains of travel? Good. Come with me, then."

Dr. Garrow led the way upstairs, turned to the left by the gallery railing, then into a short corridor on the right. He threw open the second door.

"You'll remember your way?" he said. "This is not a large house but it is possible to be confused. I think you have everything here—soap, water, towels. I shall see you again, then, in a minute, or so."

He went, closing the door behind him, and Roger, looking about him, stepped over to the wash-stand. The room was furnished with a kind of luxurious simplicity. The high oak four-poster could have given simultaneous rest to half a dozen; the great wardrobe could have held a trousseau. But the panelled walls, almost black in the shadowy places, were unadorned.
Roger took off his coat and, while washing his hands, remembered again the little parcel which Marjory Vallence had given him. As soon as his hands were dry he broke the string, tossed paper on to the bed, and opened a little cardboard box. Inside, among tissue paper, lay a silver crucifix.

He regarded it while his heart beat a little faster because of the thought behind the gift. Then the smile created by the thought of Marjory faded from his lips and he saw his eyes staring back at him from the mirror and charged with sudden and horrified conjectures.

Two fragments of recent speech returned immediately to his mind.

"Have you brought with you into the house anything which might offend a man of a certain temperament?"

"I am very susceptible to the presence of certain things, and something is causing me a great deal of discomfort."

Frowning, he put the crucifix away in an empty drawer. It was impossible, of course—that dreadful, dark suspicion in his mind. But what if it were not? What if—God help him—-it happened to be true; if the thing that Marjory had told him were true?

Two or three minutes later he knew beyond reasonable doubt. Quietly and unobtrusively the truth was set before him.

A small table in the hall had been already laid for tea. Dr. Garrow looked up as he came down the stairs and..... Dr. Garrow smiled suavely as he approached.

"Ah, that is better," he said softly. "You have left it upstairs—whatever it was that I did not like. But never mind that now. Do you take sugar and cream?"

CHAPTER VI
AND STILL MORE STRAWS

Dr. Garrow, in the act of passing Roger his cup of tea, chirruped as if he were coaxing a bird to be fed.

"I found you admiring that tapestry just now," he said with a wave of the hand. "It is a very rare piece of work, one of those rare pieces of which the market value is merely conjectural. Fourteenth century English—not Flemish—but restored in Bruges in the early seventeenth century. It is called *'Saihanus Victor'*. I cannot tell the object of the weavers. In those days they must have avowed a pious purpose, as to warn the World whither it was going. If that were so they must have found on the completion of their work an equivocal result. Look at those faces."
"I have looked at them," said Roger simply.

He looked now at Dr. Garrow's, unsure if he had seen for a fleeting moment the suspicion of a smirk. If that were so it was now smoothed out Of features which had become almost expressionless.

"I am fond of art," Dr. Garrow proceeded"—art and literature; and especially unconventional art and literature. But as regards pictures by the acknowledged masters, I have quite a pleasing although small collection scattered about the house. The one where I am pointing —the shadow catches it just at this moment—the man up there in the ruff, I mean, is by Van Dyck.

' "The subject is a Mr. Gervase, a gentleman of no great importance even in his time, but the father of a gentleman who figured in a most diverting divorce case in the days of Charles the Second. This Mr. Gervase the younger was the cause of the Duke of Norfolk divorcing his Duchess, and in the background there hovers the, shadowy figure of a certain Mistress Nelly Gwynne. I must let you read the case. I have it upstairs in the library in an old volume of state trials." '

He paused to extend a courteous hand for Roger's cup. "And speaking of my library," he continued, "brings me to mention something which I shall want you to do for me. No doubt you have been wondering what services I should wish you to perform: Well, among other things, my library needs reclassifying and cataloguing.

I mean, of course, my larger library—to which I would not mind admitting the Archbishop of Canterbury if he chanced to call. Not my smaller and intimate library— which is in my dressing-room under lock and key."

His manner seemed to invite a question. Something in Roger rebelled at going further than saying, "Yes?"

"I have books and manuscripts *there,* Mr. Moorlock" Dr. Garrow proceeded with a silky, sly satisfaction, "which, if it were proved that I had shown them to another, would procure me imprisonment for what would remain of my natural life in any country in the world— in any country, that is, with the exception of Soviet Russia and perhaps Turkey. I have spent a great deal of money—a vast deal—on books and manuscripts."

"With any particular end in view?" Roger asked.

Dr. Garrow uttered a soft, slow, secretive laugh and his eyes kindled.

"Oh, to be sure, to be sure. Although 'End' 'is perhaps not the word I should have chosen. Have you ever dreamed—idly, of course—of having unlimited wealth, and ergo, unlimited power coupled with unlimited life and therefore unlimited happiness—in *this* life, Mr. Moorbock?"

"Oh, the man's mad!" Roger was thinking; but he hid the thought behind a quiet smile which might be taken \ for cynicism rather than derision.

"Fortunately I haven't," he said with a faint laugh. "I should have wakened on some very bleak mornings during the past few months."

Dr. Garrow looked hard at him and nodded and laughed softly in his throat.

"Those who seek not," he said slowly, "will never find. And again, those who seek will find—*only if they have the courage."*

His manner changed suddenly and he rose briskly.

"Come," he said, "and I will show you the library." Roger, glad to move and glad to end the conversation, rose and followed Dr. Garrow upstairs—to a room in the western w'ing of the house. As Roger had supposed, the walls were lined with books from floor to ceiling, but his gaze, roving the shelves, failed to alight on the cover of one of well-known rarity or value. Truly an archbishop might have walked around the room and retired bored rather than shocked.

"Just take a look round at your leisure," he said, "and afterwards do as you please. Of course, I can't expect you to start work now—nor even tomorrow, if you feel like resting. It will take you a little while to shake yourself to the ways of a household which I own are somewhat peculiar. Do what you like until dinner and go where you like, except—"

He came suddenly to a pause. His voice, still suave and courteous when he resumed, yet had a warning note.

"Except—forgive me for expressing myself in a manner which I could quite understand your resenting, but you do not know me yet and I must make myself clear if even at the expense of i trifle of courtesy. When I am in my private study I am not in any circumstance— in any circumstance—to be disturbed. That is for your sake as much as mine—Moorlock."

In coming to the end of his period he hesitated and omitted the "Mr." This was a tentative overture of friendliness, and helped to rob the speech of a little of its air of despotism. Roger, who had sampled this manner from headmasters during his schoolmastering career, now found the training helpful and smoothed down his own hackles.

Alone, he sat down and lit a cigarette and tried to think. He could have no doubt that he had taken service with a very peculiar and a very evil man. But jn what ways was he evil, except in that he had lightly and freely admitted the possession of certain books? And while he was ruminating Dr. Garrow came back apd looked inside the door.

"By the way," he said, "I think I forgot to tell you. Don't trouble to dress for dinner if you are tired, or if it is in any other way inconvenient."

"I was wondering about that," Roger returned. "I don't know if my luggage has come yet. I was wondering how they were going to get it here. The gate on the drive seemed to me to be jammed."

Dr. Garrow smiled.

"Oh, yes," he said, "I keep it like that. It keeps out inquisitive people with cars who would otherwise come right up to the house pretending they had heard it was for sale or to be let. But there is a back drive, and that is the way it would come. I daresay Trode has taken it to your room. I should go and see."

He paused and turned to go.

"But I repeat—you need not put on evening clothes unless you wish. *I myself invariably wear a purple robe."* He withdrew his head from the doorway while he was making this astounding statement, giving Roger the freedom to wear what look he pleased.

Roger did not know if his smothered ejaculations were overheard; and other words came muttering from his lips.

"Good God, the man's mad! Mad as Bedlam!"

He stood still, repeating the words.

"And—is he safe?" That came next. And he fell to wondering if the deaf mute Trode were the man's keeper, until an even darker thought came to overlay it. "No, he's mad, too. They're both mad in the same way. They've something in common, those two."

Roger checked the sudden rush of thoughts. He forced a smile and addressed himself silently with a weak but helpful effort of humour.

"Steady, me lad, steady! Where's that there bull-dog courage wot we've 'eard so much about? Couldn't I take 'em both on one 'anded, if it came to *that?* I'd say I could! Funky of a pair of weak old"

He spluttered over something opprobrious.

"And I shouldn't wonder if that's the right word!" he concluded with a broad grin.

Roger walked out, whistling softly to himself, and found the way to his bedroom. His trunk had arrived and lay at the foot of the great four-poster. He took out his keys at once, opened it and, seizing armfuls of his belongings, threw them on the bed.

Some ties came to light, and these he carried over to the drawers, opening the one in which he had placed Marjory's gift. An instant later a muffled and inarticulate cry startled Roger who himself had uttered it. The drawer was empty.

He understood in a flash. Garrow the evil, Garrow the devil's servant had known—had felt what he carried in his pocket. And Garrow, or his creature, had quietly dispossessed him.

Yes, the horror of the situation lay not so much in Garrow's abhorrence of the sacred symbol as in the fact that the man *felt* that he possessed it—had known, indeed, without seeing or being told. Roger hesitated, and felt the sweat running down from his forehead. Then he did something which he had not done for years, save under school and college discipline.

But he was on his knees only for an instant and the name of God had hardly left his lips when a sudden crash jangled his taut nerves and brought him back upon his feet.

It was only a window which for no obvious reason—there being little wind astir—had suddenly blown open.

God's clean air was in the room.

CHAPTER VII
THE FIRST EVENING

Roger did not go downstairs until after a gong in the hall had rattled for the second time. Although he had been given his freedom in the matter of clothes he decided to change into a well-worn but still respectable dinner jacket; and he began to dress directly he heard the first gong.

While he stood knotting a black tie he silently questioned the troubled face in the glass. Should he mention the matter of the crucifix, or make a tacit pretence of being unaware of his loss?

After some thought, he decided on the second course. An accusation of theft— direct or implied—against somebody in the house might raise a situation which could end only by his walking out of it. And for three reasons he was anxious to stay at least a little while.

His poverty was one and his liking to be near Marjory - and her people another. The third, and perhaps not the least, was his curiosity regarding Dr. Garrow. If the man were really evil, and practising evil, he must be frustrated. Nor did he feel in the least treacherous for holding such an intention. If—and the thought now seemed a great deal less fantastic than it had seemed a few short hours ago—the man were, in plain words, in league with Darkness, all seemed fair in fighting him.

On the other hand, he was prepared to protect Dr. Garrow from anybody or anything save the law. It was obvious that he had secured the post because he was big and tough and a good boxer. Dr. Garrow, by his own words, was afraid of somebody or something; and Roger —in the spirit of the Mercenaries of another age—was willing to stand by him against any enemy outside the law.

"I wish he'd told me nothing at all," the Face in the glass was saying to Roger. "I wish nobody had told me anything, or thrown out hints. As it is, I shan't be i satisfied until I know more. And when I know more I may find it impossible to stay."

The gong presently sounded a second time and Roger went downstairs into the hall, to receive a slight shock for which he ought to have been prepared.

Dr. Garrow, robed in purple from shoulders to feet, stood beckoning at the dining-room door. He looked a little like a cardinal, a little like an alumnus of some foreign university. Roger, aware that he ought to want to laugh, was further disturbed to find that he was not in the least amused. Eccentricity, when not funny, is always malignant, and although Roger would have been amused at another's description of Dr. Garrow he could see nothing funny in the man himself.

The long oak table, laid at either end, was furnished with mats and d'oylies; and Roger was a little surprised at the array of glasses on his right hand. He counted eight of them in a diamond shaped cluster.

Trode served sherry as they sat down and then went to a dinner waggon to ladle soup.

Dr. Garrow took a spoonful and then watched his secretary with an inquiring smile.

"You like it?" he asked.

"Yes, it's excellent. I had some a little like it once in Paris, but I forget what it was called."

"You'd better ask Trode. Oh, I forgot—you can't. Anyhow he made it, and I don't think we've a name for it."

"Really?" said Roger—and brought out a question which he was not quite sure if he ought to ask. "Is he your cook?"

"He is—and a very excellent one, too, as I think you will be able to agree before long. In fact, Trode is everything."

"You mean he does all the work?"

Dr. Garrow's answer was a little cryptic.

"I mean that you're unlikely to see anybody else."

Roger wondered, thinking of the size of the house and the excellent state in which it was kept. And he wondered again when fresh salmon-trout took the place of soup. He was now prepared for almost anything in this house of surprises, but the next course consisted simply of plain roast mutton and two vegetables.

"By the way," said Dr. Garrow suddenly, "I ought to have asked you before we sat down, if you cared for caviare. It is too late now, of course, but I will remember in future, for we have plenty."

He paused, glanced at Roger and smiled. Then he continued in a tone to match the sudden playful familiarity of the words.

"And now what are you smiling at, young man? Let me share the joke."

"Well," said Roger, "you told me you don't entertain and you don't like caviare. And yet you keep it."

Dr. Garrow's next words, spoken simply and airily, provoked Roger to a sudden short laugh which he was unable quite to restrain.

"Oh, Trode likes it—Trode likes it."

And having uttered this staggering remark Dr. Garrow, smiling softly at Roger's amusement and consequent embarrassment, went on quietly with his dinner.

Roger ate and drank abstemiously. He had not much appetite for the excellent meal, nor much desire for wine. But afterwards he accepted a liqueur glass of brandy to precede the small cup of Mocha coffee.

Trode brought him cigarettes at the coffee stage, handed them on to his master, and then retired. Dr. Garrow' sipped and smoked and allowed silence for two or three minutes. Then he spoke gently across the table.

"Well, what do you feel like doing? I have a little spare time tonight. Shall we go up to the library?"

"As you please," said Roger agreeably.

"Do you play chess?"

"A little," said Roger.

He played extremely well, but this was not the time to admit it. Some warden in his inner consciousness warned him that Dr. Garrow played a great deal better. And in this, at first, he thought himself deceived; for when the game began it went in Roger's favour. Dr. Garrow lost his queen's rook and his queen's bishop.

When, however, Dr. Garrow had thus deliberately handicapped himself, as subsequently it seemed, he turned defeat into victory, slowly and in a manner which suggested inevitability. Roger looked up and smiled after he had been mated.

"Sorry I couldn't give you a better game," he said. "I suppose you are one of the masters?"

"Ye-es, but I am hardly the best living player. There are three or four men in the world who could probably beat me. I do not get much practice. Occasionally I play with Trode, but he is—forgive me—hardly better than yourself."

Roger laughed, and Dr. Garrow, rustling in his purple robe, smiled deeply and agreeably.

"Oh," he continued, "and talking of Trode I want to warn you. If you hear him scream out in the night, don't take any notice."

Roger smiled and frowned.

"Does he have nightmares?" he asked.

"Yes, you have guessed rightly at once. And poor Trode, you know he is an admirable man, but he is not quite like other men. His being unable to talk at all—except when I make him—"

"I don't understand."

"Occasionally, when I think it necessary, I hypnotize Trode. Then he develops vocal powers. But of course it is not Trode himself who uses them."

The lunatic had peeped out again, and Roger, trying to hide his thought, inquired: "Who then?"
Dr. Garrow laughed good-humouredly and gave his secretary a brief glance which was full of meaning and almost coy, and utterly repulsive.

"My dear fellow," he said, in a quiet, almost lazy tone, "I should have to know you a great deal better before I answered that question. Meanwhile," he continued more briskly, "you need not mind him. He is a good servant, entirely devoted to me and will serve you well for my sake. And now—I am not going to bed just yet, but I retire early. By the way, I hate to impose irritating restrictions, but I want you to be in your room every night by ten-thirty. I want them to feel that the house is locked up and everything quiet."

Roger inclined his head.

"I generally retire pretty early in any case," he said, "and I'm generally up early. By the way, at what times will you want me? I mean, I shall need a certain amount of exercise—"

"Oh, I don't mind. Your time, within certain broad limits, will be your own. I expect you'd like to go out for a stroll shortly before eleven in the morning."

This suited Roger so exactly that he smiled.

"There is," Dr. Garrow continued off-handedly, "a very nice-looking girl in the neighbourhood. A Miss Vallence, the vicar's daughter."

Roger drew a quick breath and bit his lip.

"Oh?" he grunted. "Why?"

"I was thinking that if you went out about then you would probably meet her. But—especially coming from this house—you might find it a little difficult to get an introduction to her." He paused and added very gently: *"Unless you know her already* In a flash Roger remembered Marjory's words: *"He knows you're talking to me now."* He stared at Dr. Garrow, dismay looking through the mask of his face.

"It happens that I *do* know her," he muttered. "I was at school with her brother. I've only met her about twice."

"Ah! You did not mention that to me."

"I did not see the necessity."

Dr. Garrow inclined his head and presently spoke in a mild and self-consciously reasonable tone.

"Well, Moorlock, your friends are no affair of mine. Meet them and go to the Vicarage whenever you please. I don't think you will induce them to come here, but you may try. But remember this—for your own sake, if we are to continue friends—I do not care to be discussed."

"No," said Roger, "but it will be a little difficult to avoid mentioning you at all."

"You know what I mean," said Dr. Garrow simply. There was a short pause. Then Dr. Garrow smote his palms swiftly together and rubbed them briskly as if the acts dispelled something uncomfortable which had crept into the atmosphere.

"And now good-night, Moorlock," he said, in a tone which almost suggested reconciliation after a quarrel. "I am going to retire now. You will be in your room by ten-thirty?"

"Well, I think I'll take a book and go straight there. Anyhow, I'm not fond of late hours."

"Wise fellow. Beauty sleep. Look at *me.* And I'm a great deal—a very great deal older than you'd guess."

CHAPTER VIII
A CRY IN THE NIGHT

Roger, entering his sanctuary—as he hoped to call it— with a book in his hand, turned at once to ascertain something which, in a private house, had never previously concerned him. He found that there was a lock on the door, but no key within or without, and this small omission brought a frown to his forehead.

One does not generally lock one's door in private houses, but nevertheless the key is almost invariably there. Nor could he ask for a key, however tactfully, without making an insulting innuendo. He could imagine the Doctor's suave but pained reply.

"Why, Moorlock, what do you want with a key? There is only Trode besides myself, and I can assure you that Trode is unlikely to disturb you."

He could, of course, complain that the crucifix was missing; but he was singularly unwilling to mention his loss. A thought occurred to him and he went over to the chest of drawers. But the crucifix had not been returned, and he pushed back the drawer with a sense of desolation.
He felt in some manner trapped—in an out of the way and hitherto undreamed of meaning of the word. He was reminded of an incident of his school life—Blindfold Boxing on the last night of a term. He had not known who was his opponent, nor seen whence the blows came; and when his own blows landed by chance he could not see where or with what effect. Some of that sensation was back upon him now; but without the laughter on his own lips and the yelling uproar of convulsed spectators.

He sat and read for an hour, but he was in the mood to find any book dull, and the one which eventually he laid aside had suffered unjustly in his esteem. So he undressed and got into bed.
A miniature step-ladder of mahogany—four steps with a little strip of carpet upon each—stood beside the bed; but he disdained the means by which dignified little ladies and unathletic gentlemen had reached the reposeful altitude two centuries before. His body sank deep, as he had guessed it would, and he grunted his discontent; for he hated feather beds.

But while he lay thinking the unpleasant smother in which he wallowed gave him an idea. Tomorrow he would look around for a room in which there was a bed with a spring mattress; and—having first annexed the key of the door—he would ask permission to change his room, urging the mattress as an excuse.

Garrow could scarcely object to his making the change; and, with regard to the key, Garrow would find it as awkward to question him as now he found it awkward to question Garrow. Put into a better humour by his own simple subtlety— for it is good for a man at times to fancy himself a knowing fellow and a' deep schemer—Roger became more in the mood for slumber. He had closed his eyes and was on the twilight frontier when he took a sudden backward leap to wide-eyed consciousness, his nerves tingling, his intaken breath as cold as frosty air. He sat bolt upright as the scream reached its climax and suddenly gave way to its own echoes.

He had been warned, and he was prepared for a disturbance on this or any night. But no such cry as that. He had had no experience of somnambulists and he could imagine a shout of amazement and fear from a man suddenly wakened in strange surroundings. But this surely was a cry of agony, a death-cry, the inarticulate farewell of body to soul.

Roger leaped out of bed and, forgetting its height from the floor, came crashing on hands and
knees. The sound of his own fall robbed his ears of the ring of echoes, and in this momentary confusion he lost the direction whence the cry had sounded. But he was sure that it came from somewhere within the house—from a distance but still somewhere within the walls.

He scrambled to the door, flung it open and ran down the passage, shouting; and still shouting he reached the stairhead. There he paused, not knowing which direction to take. He stood still for a minute, continuing to shout and straining his ears for an answer. And an answer came suddenly as light from below leaped up like a stage effect through the well of the staircase.

"Yes? What's the matter?"

It was Dr. Garrow's voice, cold and irascible. Roger ran to the stairhead and down the stairs to see, as he turned the angle, Dr. Garrow standing below. Roger came running down. "Are you all right?" he called.

"Yes, of course." Garrow's face had lost its pink complexion and was now yellow-white. "Why are you making all the fuss? Didn't I warn you about Trode?"

"That was never Trode!"

"I tell you it was!" Dr. Garrow's irascibility was made manifest in cold, rapid speech. "I warned you not to take any notice, and now you come rushing—"

Roger continued downstairs and faced him. Garrow seemed to be mastering his temper and laid a hand on Roger's sleeve.

"I am very sorry," he said, with half a laugh. "It seems that I did not make it sufficiently clear to you as to what a nuisance Trode can be when the sleep-walking fit is on him. Often I am able to walk him back to his room without waking him, but sometimes—as tonight— he comes to with a severe shock, and announces his return to full consciousness in the manner which you have just heard."

Roger laughed, ashamed of himself for feeling—and doubtless looking—shaken.

"That's all very well," he said, "but please be good enough to remember what you said to me in town. You hinted that you might be in danger and asked if you could rely on me. What would you have said to me if I had stayed in bed?"

Garrow eyed him, nodded twice and grinned, as if tacitly conceding the point.

"Yes," he said, "I beg your pardon. But now you have heard Trode at his worst—or very nearly his worst—and not the kind of noise I might make if in danger or even in *extremis.* I think I could contrive at best a reasonable shout—although I suppose one never knows. Well, thank you; and now take my advice and go back to bed." He paused and smiled again.

"I am sorry if you have been startled, but perhaps it was as well that you had the experience so soon. If you hear the same kind of uncanny din again you will be able to turn over and go to sleep again."

Roger smiled as if he doubted it, and Dr. Garrow smiled too in speaking.

"Well, good-night once more. I don't think you will be disturbed again."

Back in his bed once more, Roger lay thinking. The thoughts were macabre and contradictory; but in the midst of them sleep came suddenly to hide all under a black cloth—which he lifted hours later to show the mullioned windows aglow and motes playing in long angled sunbeams.
He was hardly aware of being awake when he heard a tap at the door and Trade entered with a laden tea-tray.

"Oh, thanks," said Roger, forgetting the man's infirmity; and as he sat up he wondered how long it would take him to remember that it was useless to speak to Trode unless Trode was closely watching his lips.

But Trode had something more than merely the tea. It was a scrap of paper with pencilled writing on it. This he held up pointedly for Roger to take and read. Roger did so. The note, presumably addressed to himself, was a very short one.

"I *am sorry, sir, if I startelled you last night. I cant help it sometimes.*
Yrs Respectfully.
WILLIAM TRODE."

Roger smiled and nodded to show that he understood and appreciated and a faint answering smile appeared for a moment on the white face. Then" the deaf-mute turned abruptly and went quietly out.

Daylight not only dispels the darkness of the world but the darkness of the mind. Roger, sipping his tea, was disposed to smile at the recent happening in darkness. He reflected, not without grim amusement, that Trode was well equipped with lungs and that it was wrong to call him dumb. Inarticulate, perhaps, but certainly not dumb.

Then he rose, took towels and went down to the bathroom near at hand, checking himself in his own doorway to save himself from tripping over the can of hot water on the mat.

There was a reason for the hot water, as he soon discovered, for both taps in the bath ran cold. It meant taking a cold bath and returning to his room to shave. This he did, and he was in the act of unscrewing his safety razor when he saw a red stain at the end of the left sleeve of his pyjama jacket.

He had cut himself before, and rather badly, with a safety razor; and his gaze went back to the mirror as he lifted and stretched his chin. But his skin seemed to be intact and the drying remains of lather were white.

Roger glanced again at his sleeve which he had dampened with his wet fingers. The blood seemed fresher now, and set him frowning again. But it was not the first time that he had cut himself and failed to find the abrasion and the incident passed out of his mind until, while dressing, he went over and stood by the high bed.

In the act of rising from it he had bared the top sheet, and now he saw on it a small, faint smear which looked, like blood. This set him running fingers reflectively through his hair. It argued that he had cut or scratched himself on the preceding night before retiring to bed, but he could neither think of the cause nor find any damage done to his skin.

The incident—trivial as it seemed at the time—was gone from his mind a moment or two later. Within ten minutes he was on his way downstairs, wondering where breakfast would be served. He was not long in doubt, for almost at once he observed a table laid in the hall and Trode bending above it in the act of setting down a cover.

The man looked up, warned of Roger's approach by the vibrations of his footfalls, and pointed to a small urn and then to a coffee pot, both of which stood upon the table. Roger understood and pointed to the coffee pot, and Trode departed carrying the urn.

The table was laid only for one. Evidently Dr. Garrow breakfasted in his own room if he breakfasted at all. There was no morning paper, nor any signs of a mail. Roger sat down, his back to the tapestry. He did not like *Sathanus Victor,* but its presence did not destroy his appetite.

So he sat in filtered sunlight, eating and enjoying breakfast, while behind him the eternal procession to Hell went by upon the shadowed wall.

CHAPTER IX
A WORD FROM THE POLICE

After breakfast Roger went upstairs to the library to begin part of his sketchily defined duties. He had never before tried to catalogue a library; and this one, although neat enough to the eye, became chaotic upon close insection.

Going from left to right along a shelf he found Burton's *"Anatomy " "Macbeth," "Barnaby Rudge,"* one volume of the *Essays* of Oliver Wendel Holmes, an odd volume of Figuer, Daudet's *"Lettres de mon Moulin"* and a handbook on gardening, all standing cheek by jowl. No doubt Garrow had some private system in this lack of system by which he knew more or less where to set his, hand upon any given book; but it remained for Roger to find out what books he had before attempting to separate them into categories.

The shelves were all lettered and numbered, and a ledger, a stack of cards and writing materials had been placed for Roger on a desk. There evidently was the task and it remained for him to do it.

He sat down and thought it out, feeling absurdly like a character in some fairy-tale—one who had fallen into the power of a witch and could ransom himself only by the performance of some impossible feat. It was pleasant in one sense, although not encouraging in another, to feel that Garrow did not care how he did his work, or whether he did it at all.

After a while he began to evolve a system. There must be English and foreign sections, the foreign section again divided into languages, and the whole subdivided again into Plays and Poetry, Fiction, Essays, Scientific Works—more sub-divisions here—and Miscellany. More than once he sent a glance, of half-amused apprehension at the library ladder of polished cedar and wondered how many times he was doomed to pass up and down.

Meanwhile, the audible ticking of a heavy clock was a constant reminder of the passing of time, and mindful of Garrow's permission to work and leave work when he chose, he allowed the evolution of the new system to be suspended directly the clock struck the half hour after ten. Five minutes later he was out of the house and on his way down the drive.

He was reminded at once of the red-haired sailor with the burnished face whom he had encountered on the previous afternoon, and wondered how that happy-go-lucky son of the sea was faring—if he had come safely to port in his Warwickshire home, or if he had fallen foul of any more of those rocks and shoals which beset the course of the sailor man ashore. Already he had half forgotten the man's face and little dreamed on that morning of sun and shade how vividly—and horribly—it would glide back into the light of memory.

He reached the post-office before he was due, but he was not too early. In the middle distance a gloved hand fluttered for a moment above a hat of cornflower blue; and he went hurrying towards Marjory Vallence. She approached him slowly, and with a little smile, as if she knew that his heart was jogging faster than his feet.

"It's wonderful!" she said by way of greeting.

"Yes, isn't it?" he agreed laughing. "Fancy a girl being punctual! Even a bit better than punctual."

"No—I meant about the ogre letting you off the chain. I hardly expected to see you. Anyhow, I'm afraid I haven't got long. Mater wants me. Well?"

"Well—what?"

"Tell me. How do you like—er—everything and all that? You know what I mean."

He laughed.

I "You don't like mentioning the unholy name. Oh, he's all right, I think. Certainly unusual. I don't know whether I ought to talk about him much." He paused and laughed—this time a little awkwardly. "I'm eating his grub and removing a little of his surplus cash."

She made a little shocked gesture.

"Oh, don't be a gentlemanly gentleman. Nobody is to-day. I know what it is. You're afraid he'll know I exactly what you're saying. And I believe you're right."

"Well, the odd thing is that he seemed to know I met you yesterday—before I told him."

Marjory looked at him with a meaning smile and nodded.

"Yes," she said simply, "didn't I warn you?"

"And I can't think how he knew, because I don't see who could have told him in the house."

The girl was laughing as one laughs at the mysterious.

"Well, I told you! The man's uncanny—and unholy. What did he say?"

"Nothing. I mean he was just ordinary. Except that he said he didn't want to be discussed. He was pretty urgent about that; but, as he might have known, it's unavoidable. Doesn't seem to mind my going to the Vicarage—if your people are good enough to let me. But he said he thought "it unlikely that they would pay a return visit. I'm just wondering what's wrong with him."

Her eyes suddenly narrowed.

"My dear Roger, Father's told you and I've told you. We all know. You—hasn't he dropped *you* a hint?" Roger was silent a moment, wondering how he should answer.

"He's certainly talked rather wildly," he agreed.

He was debating in his mind how much and how little to tell her. His loyalty to Garrow, due from a paid servant, and his wishing to spare the girl anxiety for her brother's friend, were pulling him in the same direction. Before he could continue, she brought out a point-blank question.

"Have you still got what I gave you?"

He was prepared for it, and had his answer ready. It seemed to him that he could do no good by telling her the truth. Retold at the Vicarage it would pass as confirmation of a ghastly suspicion and raise a mountain of anxiety on his behalf. He brought out his white lie flatly, and continued rapidly, in the manner of those who are not used to lapsing from the truth.

"Of course, and—forgive me—I ought to have thanked you before. That was—er—an awfully nice thought, Marjory."

Feminine intuition seemed to fail her here.

"Oh, I'm glad. Father was afraid he'd know, and make you get rid of it, or else take it away. Steal it, I mean. But I suppose he was afraid. Well—I'm glad."

She smiled again and changed her tone.

"And now, young Master Roger, what about it?"

"Sorry," he answered smiling, "but I can't always read people's thoughts. That's why I'm not shunned."

"When are you coming to see us? Tea. Tennis. Got a racket with you?"

"To tell you the truth a bad fairy got hold of it and turned it into a pawn-ticket."

"Well, Reggie left one behind. Rather like a landing- net. But quite good enough for you when you're playing against me. This afternoon? Tomorrow?"

He laughed.

"Oh, thanks very much, but may I leave it open, if you'll be in both days? I've hardly done any work yet. I say—is that big chap on the other side of the road waiting to talk to you?"

She looked up and her expression changed.

"Oh, that's the Inspector."

"School or Nuisances?"

"Police," laughed Marjory. "He's been to see us before. About that—you know—that grave. I think he—Excuse me just for a moment."

She had caught the large man's glance and seen a slow tentative pace taken in her direction.

With that she left Roger's side and walked across the road towards the large man in blue serge who took a quickened step or two in her direction.

Roger turned away, but looked up again a minute later when he heard light and heavy footfalls crossing the road towards him.

"Oh, Mr. Moorlock," it was Marjory's voice addressing him formally in the Inspector's presence.

"Can you spare a minute? Mr. Stillby would like to speak to you. Well, I must hurry. Goodbye. We shall see you this afternoon or tomorrow, then?"

Her own haste necessitated the brevity of Roger's goodbye. The Inspector's "Sorry to trouble you, sir" cut through it. He eyed Roger politely, but appraisingly, and began at once.

"I'm making inquiries connected with the desecration of that grave—the late Mr. Thurley's grave—and the removal of the coffin containing the body."

"Yes," said Roger.

"And I understand that you are Dr. Garrow's secretary. I took the liberty of asking the young lady who you might be."

"That is quite right," said Roger, "but I am afraid I cannot help you. I arrived only yesterday."

"Ah!" The Inspector succeeded in looking as if he had not already known. "Well, you'll be seeing Dr. Garrow soon?"

"When I return, I daresay. But I can't be sure."

"Well, he's not on the telephone, and I've written to say I was coming, and I've called twice. But I can't get any sense out of that deaf and dumb man of his. He's given me to understand that Dr. Garrow's been out on both occasions and he hasn't been able to let me know when Dr. Garrow's going to be in."

"I see," said Roger, non-committally but thoughtfully. "So will you kindly tell Dr. Garrow that I am calling on him at three o'clock this afternoon and I hope he will make it convenient to be at home. If he can't, will you tell him that I must see him immediately—to-day if possible—either here or at the Station in Reading."

"Certainly I'll tell him."

"Thank you. I understand that he's a scholarly gentleman who doesn't like to be disturbed, but kindly tell him that it is necessary for me to see him and that I intend to see him."

Roger smiled, but not derisively. There was a firmness and fixity of purpose in the manner which commanded respect.

"Very well—I'll give him your message," he said.

CHAPTER X
THE INSPECTOR CALLS

Roger, on his way back, found a great deal for thought and not a little for private amusement. That Dr. Gar- row would resent the threatened intrusion seemed certain; but there remained the problem as to whether he would deliberately avoid it.

Could the Police force themselves upon a man in order to try to extract information from him whether he possessed such information or not? Roger doubted it. The most he imagined they could do would be to subpoena the object of their interest to give evidence in court or at coroner's inquiry. If that were the case—and Dr. Garrow undoubtedly knew his own position—what was to happen next?

There was a certain piquancy in the situation amounting almost to excitement. If Dr. Garrow continued to deny himself to the Police, as Roger half expected, what would be their next move? And if he permitted the interview what would he have to say? Irked by a curiosity pardonable enough in the circumstances, Roger wondered if subsequently he would ever hear what took place.

Back at the house he made pencilled inquiry of Trode and I learned that Dr. Garrow was in his private sanctum, in which he must not be disturbed. Roger thought that the time had come for breaking one of the rules. He wrote a pencilled note, inscribed *"Urgent"* and gave it to Trode, who took it unwillingly. It brought Dr. Garrow into the library ten minutes later. Anger burned in his eyes and tightened the corners of his mouth.

"What," he asked coldly, "is the meaning of this?"

"I think it explains itself," said Roger, slightly resentful.

"Why didn't you tell the man I couldn't see him?"

"I had no authority to do that. Your own authority, I mean. And had I done so it could have served no useful purpose."

"What do you mean?"

"If the police want to see you they will do so. I don't think the most exclusive privacy is considered in matters of urgency or public policy."

Dr. Garrow's lips writhed impatiently.

"Urgency? Public policy? What do they think I can tell them about that old fool? I was only on bare speaking terms with him. He was a fool in life and he seems to have been a fool in death—even to the extent of losing his own carrion."

As he looked at Roger's face his expression changed a little, as if he suddenly repented his last utterance.

"It is not your fault," he continued, "and I am not blaming you, but I am naturally irritated. I have had no dealings with the police, but I have read enough to make me distrustful. I do not want to be forced to say things from which innuendos can be extracted. I can tell them nothing which they do not already know. But I will see the man if I must, and you will kindly be present at the interview. It is just as well to have an independent witness on such an occasion."

"Oh, certainly," said Roger.

Dr. Garrow nodded twice and continued in an easier tone

"You'll see him when he calls. Give him a chair in the hall and a cigarette and a drink if he wants them, and Trode will come and fetch me. By the way, I shall be lunching in my own room, but Trode will look after you. Make him understand any time when you want anything by way of refreshment."

"Thank you," said Roger.

Dr. Garrow smiled and turned towards the door.

"We shall meet again at about three o'clock then. Very well."

Roger continued his work in the library until lunch time—but slowly, because of distractions—and went up again afterwards until the clock told him it was ten minutes to three. Then he went down into the hall and sat there, smoking a cigarette, until the tolling of the great bell in the servants' quarters synchronized with three chimes from an adjacent clock. Inspector Stillby,
it seemed, had all the regard of his kind for punctuality.

Trode admitted him and Roger rose to receive him.

"Good afternoon, sir," began Stillby; and his gaze, travelling about him like a searchlight at sea, came to rest upon the *Salhanus Victor* tapestry. "Good Lord!" he said.

"Yes, it is a little striking," said Roger, smiling.

"Striking? Well, yes, that's about the word. Where's the Doctor?"

"He'll be down presently. The man has gone to fetch him."

"Oh, he *is* going to see me, then? I'm glad of that. It may save a lot of trouble in the long run. No, I won't smoke or drink, sir. Never do when I'm on duty. You're only just come here, sir?"

"Yes, I arrived only yesterday."

"Ah! May I ask—just out of curiosity, like—how you got in touch with Dr. Garrow?"

"Through an agency. He wanted a secretary and I wanted to be a secretary."

"I see. Not through the Vicar or his young lady?" The excellent man gave Roger a knowing look. "It hasn't taken you very long to make friends, sir."

"Good heavens!" exclaimed Roger, both annoyed and amused.

For the moment, as under glass, he could see the workings of the Inspector's mind. , Roger, the man was thinking, had just made Marjory's acquaintance that morning by the simple process of smiling at her and doffing his hat—a method not unknown at the seaside, but uncommon with the daughters of the clergy when at home in a small and censorious village.

"I happened to know the Vicar and his family," he said in a smothered voice. "I was at school with the young lady's brother."

"So your coming to live down here was just a coincidence?"

"That's right," said Roger, no longer able to see the workings of the Inspector's mind.

"Coincidence," the Inspector mused. "Ah, the world's full of them. *Real* ones, some of them, too. Now this Dr. Garrow—excuse me asking—I know he doesn't practise, but is he a doctor of medicine?"

"I believe so. Why?"

"Because there's several sorts. One of our men—his own family doctor was away, and he wanted one in a hurry one night. He'd heard of Dr. Higginbotham living not far off, so he rushes round and gets hold of the bell and doesn't leave go. At last the doctor came down and heard what poor old Bob had got to tell him, and he didn't half go off the deep end. Wanted to know what the hell a Doctor of Music was supposed to do at a confinement."

Stillby caught Roger smiling and suddenly lowered his voice.

"What's the Doctor's real work?"

"Scientific—I believe. But you must ask him yourself. I have nothing to do with it. At present I am re-arranging his library for him."

While Roger was answering, the Inspector's roving gaze focussed on the staircase, and he rose, looking over Roger's head.

"Good afternoon, Doctor," he said, as Roger turned.

Dr. Garrow came down swiftly and silently into the hall. Rather to Roger's surprise he was smiling easily, and he nodded to Stillby as he moved quietly towards him.

"Good afternoon, Inspector. Do sit down. What can I do for you?"

Stillby sat down and threw a meaning glance at Roger.

"I wanted to have a private talk with you, sir."

"By all means. Yes?"

"You don't mind this gentleman being present, sir?"

"On the contrary. I want him."

The Inspector proceeded to ignore Roger.

"As I suppose you can guess, Dr. Garrow, I am making inquiries about the desecration of the late Mr. Thurley's grave and the unauthorised removal of the body and the coffin. I was considering if you could help me. I think you knew the late Mr. Thurley, sir?"

"That would be an exaggeration. We were just on nodding and speaking terms."

"You can throw no light on what has just happened?"

"I do not see how."

"What did you think of him? Suppose for a moment, sir, I was not a police officer. How would you answer that question?"

"Oh, I should say to anyone else what I say to you. He was undoubtedly mad."

"Yet he patented some very clever inventions, sir."

"Why, yes. And you in turn must have heard that very often there is hardly a split hair between genius and lunacy.' They have the common factor of the abnormal brain."

The Inspector paused.

"Very good, sir. But can you give me any reason— any concrete reason—for calling him mad?"

"Certainly," said Dr. Garrow. "You have heard what he was working on before he died? Alchemy. A bogus science abandoned in the middle ages. An attempt to turn baser metals into gold. He made no direct claim, I believe, but dropped hints that he had succeeded in doing this. That gold poker, of his—you've seen it, I suppose—was a lunatic's jest. After his death he wanted people to believe that he had succeeded, but allowed the secret to die with him for the sake of humanity. The world would be in a terribly chaotic state for a time if everybody could turn his kitchen poker into gold."

Dr. Garrow eyed Roger and the Inspector in turn as if seeking for smiles. The Inspector responded and the twinkle was still in his eye.

"You think he said something about his secret dying with him, and we do know that he caused certain papers to be buried with him. You think then that the motive of those who desecrated his grave was to discover his alleged secret?"

Dr. Garrow shrugged his shoulders.

"I don't know. I think possibly. I say so because I can't think of any other motive. It would be useless to ask me who I think could have committed such a foolish crime, nor what has become of the body. That will doubtless come to light and furnish its own clues. I think I have heard or read somewhere that the problem of the secret disposal of the human body is well nigh insoluble."

"Ye-es," murmured Stillby. "By the way, sir, I've forgotten to inquire. How long had Mr. Thurley been living here?"

"I couldn't say."

"He was already here when you bought the property?

"Oh, yes."

"You knew him before you came to live here?"

"I had just met him. Twice in London, I think, at public dinners. And of course down here at rare and accidental meetings we just nodded. He was a valetudinarian and so, to a great extent, am I."

"A vally?"

"Hermits, Inspector, hermits," Dr. Garrow translated. "The subjects, I daresay, of much local curiosity. Well, one hermit is gone—in a double sense of the word—and left a mystery behind him. So naturally you approach the survivor, hoping that he can help you to solve it. I am afraid I am the last person in the world. Since I rarely go out, I daresay I saw even less of him than other people. I am afraid that that is all that I can tell you."

The Inspector lowered his head and coughed.

"Just one more question, Dr. Garrow," he said. "It's just a personal one and you might turn round and tell me that it isn't my business. It seems you've gone on for a long time without a secretary, and it seems you engaged this gentleman immediately after that grave had been disturbed. Were you nervous of living alone—or almost alone?"

Dr. Garrow smiled.

"You have very nearly hit the nail, although 'nervous' is not quite the word I should have used. I also have my secrets, Inspector, although my field of research is very different from the dream El Dorado in which poor Thurley laboured. Since apparently people do not stop short of robbing a grave it occurred to me that an elderly man like myself, living alone with another elderly man—and one deaf and dumb at that—was in a precarious position in the event of robbery and possible violence.

"In any event I had been realising my need for a secretary and a librarian, and it is just possible—although even I could not say for certain—that the recent turn of events caused me suddenly to make up my mind."

"Yes," said the Inspector, getting suddenly upon his legs, "I think you were wise. Thank you, sir, and I am sorry to have troubled you. Just one thing more, sir."

"Yes? Well?"

"I mayn't have to trouble you again over this affair. Or on the other hand I may. I don't know yet. I have had some difficulty in seeing you. Would you be kind enough to make it a bit easier on any future occasion?" Dr. Garrow hesitated for a moment, still smiling, but with a deepening of lines just apparent in his forehead.

"Very well," he said at last. "Come again if you think it really necessary. But write to me first and make an appointment. My work is highly concentrated and interruptions are very vexatious. I too am seeking something, Inspector—in another field."

CHAPTER XI
TEA AND TALK

Dr. Garrow saw the Inspector out, closed the great door with a soft slam and returned to Roger wearing the ghost of a weary smile and an air of boredom.

"The police," he remarked, "are all very well in their way—but their way is peculiar. They are excellent at securing the convictions of delinquent motorists and those who harbour dogs without licenses. They can often arrest burglars and murderers—if the malefactor's worst enemy knows and gives him away. Indeed they expect that, and take little trouble. But because somebody steals a corpse—which all Christians and most pagans agree is of no value in itself—they make as much fuss as if the Crown Jewels had been stolen."

Roger felt that he had to make some remark.

"It's an unusual sort of crime," he said simply.

"Yes, nowadays. And of course everybody is afraid of the unusual. And now, my good Moorlock, what were you thinking of doing?

Roger, of course, had been thinking of going to the Vicarage; but he realised that it was a little late. It would be better to go earlier on the morrow and spend a longer afternoon. He was also aware that it would look better if he went back to his work in the library. There he had been set no easy task for a man unused to that sort of work.

"There is plenty to do upstairs," he said smiling, "and I had been wondering how to begin, or rather where to begin. But I've made a start and I shall manage. Will you be wanting any books just yet?"

Dr. Garrow smiled and shook his head.

"Not from there. Just now I am very busy. Well, as I think I told you, take your time. I shall see you at dinner."

They parted. An hour later Trode, unasked by Roger, brought a tea-tray to the library; and as Roger paused to pour himself out a cup he suddenly fell to pondering a new problem.

Was Trode the only servant? He had seen no others, heard of no others. Was Trode cook, butler, footman, valet and housemaid—a composite person like the shipwrecked survivor, turned cannibal, in the ballad by Gilbert? But—here was the strange thing—the house was as well kept as if a dozen servants worked in it under the eyes of a martinet housekeeper. This was another mystery, although a small one, which had begun to tease him and would continue to do so until he discovered how it was all contrived. He remembered—with a certain curiosity not unmixed with discomfort—Garrow's remark about Trode being the only servant he was likely to see.

The opportunity came at dinner. Trode, having served the soup, had departed for a while, and Dr. Garrow, glancing across at Roger, said:

"Would you care for some more? There is plenty here on the dinner waggon. The excellent Trode is foraging in the cellar."

"No, thank you," said Roger, and laughed. "The excellent Trode, as you say, Dr. Garrow. He must be a man in a million."

"He is, of course, but why?"

"The way he runs this house. I think you told me that he was the only servant."

"I did not. I said he was the only servant that you would be likely to see."

"I don't understand," said Roger simply.

"No? No?" Garrow's voice was soft and quiet. "I am not meaning to rebuke you. Don't think that. Your curiosity is quite natural and' requires no apology. But —I hope you will not be too urgent in asking questions." The mild rebuke annoyed Roger more than a direct in-junction to mind his own business.

"Excuse me," he said, "but my position is obviously an awkward one. Suppose I meet strangers about th premises—possibly at night—"

Dr. Garrow interrupted him, speaking sharply.

"What makes you say that?"

"How am I to know if they are servants or intruders?"

Dr. Garrow's eyes narrowed and he paused over his reply.

"In the unlikely event of your seeing anybody," he said at last, "it would be an intruder. Call me. Don't make an attack."

"I still don't understand. You gave me to suppose that you had enemies and asked if I would stand by you."

Dr. Garrow uttered a little soft, patient laugh—almost the laugh of one explaining to a child not old enough to understand.

"I am sorry," he said, "that I haven't made myself clear. If I call you it will be another matter. But please forgive me if I seem mysterious, and put yourself in the place of a soldier. You have been in the O.T.C., I suppose?"

"Yes," said Roger, with a faint smile. "The soldier is supposed to do nothing without orders. And then, when he doesn't get any, he is cursed for not having used his own initiative."
Dr. Garrow laughed.

"You will not find me quite so unreasonable as that. And I think you are beginning to understand me."

Roger's face was expressionless, but he felt a kind of equivocal amusement at this easy assumption. He was further than ever from understanding the man—and the man knew it. Moreover, he was conscious of a certain helplessness in spite of his youth and strength and, he supposed, an average courage. Further to puzzle him came the thought that Dr. Garrow had need, or thought he might have need, of that courage and strength.

They did not play chess that night. Either it did not please Dr. Garrow to slaughter one unworthy of his steel or he had work to do. When he had smoked one cigarette after dinner he rose and bade Roger good-night.

"You have everything you want?" he-asked courteously. "I hope Trode will not rouse us again. Anyhow, you will know next time the kind of noise he makes."

He smiled and went. At a quarter to ten Roger went softly upstairs to his bedroom, where he sat reading for an hour. He was sleepy by then and yet curiously unwilling to go to bed. Roger knew exactly why he was unwilling to clamber up on to that great bed and lie down in the dark. The revelation came to him with a little shock which was followed by a qualm of self-disgust.

He was afraid of something. That ugly and humiliating fact came to him doubly barbed, bringing with it a sting of shame. "This isn't my real form," he said to himself. "I've never been a funk. If only I knew what was going on in this house—if anything queer is going on. It's the Unknown always, I suppose, that gets a man down. And, damn it, I wish I knew who does the housework here, or how it gets done."

He must have been debating these things when he feil suddenly asleep, to wake in the light of a dull day with Trode knocking upon his door. The silent man brought him tea and a letter.
The handwriting on the envelope was Marjory's. He had slipped his little finger inside the fold to tear it open when the fold lifted as if the gum had not taken hold.

There was very little in the letter except a certain unexpressed anxiety on his behalf.

"Sorry you couldn't come to-day, but don't forget tomorrow. Shall really expect you then. Have borrowed quite a good racket for you; and as Colonel Streatley doesn't often play I think I shall forget to give it back to him—unless he asks for it. So we shall be seeing you. But if you're not well or anything *please* let us know."

Roger smiled to himself, but the smile faded before the thought that Marjory and her people were really concerned about him. A frown followed when—idly at first—he examined the envelope. The gum was wet and the flap was limp and slightly moist.

He knew, or thought he knew, the cause. The letter had been opened with the aid of steam. Anger and amusement contended for a time before anger got the mastery.

This was really too much. Yet he had already kept silent with regard to a more serious matter, the loss of his crucifix. Again came the thought that to complain might force a crisis leading to a hurried and angry departure and he was more than ever determined to stay.

He lay and thought, raising himself from time to time to sip his tea. He had the average man's abjection to a tampering with his correspondence, but on the other hand he was unlikely to receive any that demanded secrecy.

But the possibility remained, and the simplicity of the solution—at least as regards the Vallances—made him smile as, at last, he got out of bed and seized his towel.

He breakfasted alone, went to his work in the library, and afterwards lunched alone. Garrow he did not expect to see before the evening, and indeed he had no glimpse of him all day. After lunch he changed into flannels and later in the afternoon set out for the Vicarage. On the way he called at a little shop where stationery could be bought and made a purchase which brought a brief smile to his lips as he stepped out on to the path.

The Vicarage was a large one—too large for most of its incumbents during the past two hundred and thirty years. It was built of red brick and had the doll's house symmetry of most Queen Anne houses. Marjory had evidently seen him approach, for she opened the door and came down to meet him on the drive.

"Hullo!" she called. "You got my note all right?"

"Yes, thanks. At least—I *got* it."

"What do you mean?"

"Nothing. I've got a small present for you. By the way, has Mr. Vallence got anything on one of his little fingers? I haven't noticed."

"Anything on—?"

"Anything bearing the family crest, I mean. Anyhow, I got you this in case there isn't any in the house." While speaking he handed her a stick of red sealing wax. She took it and understood at once. A little sharp exclamation followed.

"Oh! You don't mean to say that man?"

"I can't be quite sure, but I've a nasty strong suspicion. Way the envelope came open."

She looked at him, her lips apart as if for utterance, but a moment or two elapsed before she spoke.

"Didn't I tell you that that man—"

"Yes; in league with the devil," he said lightly; for at the moment it suited him to take that tone.
"Well, a penn'orth of sealing wax does the devil in the eye. I hope to be seeing you so often that there won't be much need to write. But if the occasion arises—"

He paused and smiled again.

"Yes?"

"I hardly like to suggest it, because it costs threepence extra."

"Do you mean register it?"

"That's the idea. Good scheme registration. Well, how's everybody?"

"They're all right. Still a bit worried about you. Don't know where they are at the moment. They'll be about presently. Like a game?"

"Thanks."

They went on to the tennis court behind the house and had played half a set when Mrs. Vallence suddenly appeared. After a ten minutes halt they went on playing until the tea-bell tinkled from an open window in the house.

The Vicar was in the drawing-room when they arrived. He greeted Roger with a smile which was eloquent of unspoken thought.

"Hullo, Roger. Glad to see you. Still alive, then?"

"Yes—although Marjory's been making me run about."

"Court playing all right?"

"Yes, thanks."

Vallence laughed.

"Don't thank me. Marjory mowed and rolled it this morning. We've lost our part-time gardener."

"I'm sorry about that." Roger sat at Mrs. Vallence's tacit invitation. "You don't mean he's dead."
"No, but he's been drunk for the last two or three days. Whether I shall take him back depends on the apparent sincerity of his repentance. Also I don't know who else to get—and that may weigh with me."

The Vicar paused and laughed.

"What puzzles me—although it's no affair of mine— is where he got the money. I've been paying him eighteen bob a week, and he's been picking up about as much again from other people. Now how much does it cost to get drunk on gin?"

"Thomas!" said Mrs. Vallence.

"A purely academic question, my dear, and—er—not put to you. I was asking Roger."

"Thank you," said Roger, when the laugh had subsided. "I hate gin anyhow. I suppose it depends on the individual capacity. I daresay a man could train up to two or three bottles a day. A persevering man, I mean."

"Well, that would come to twenty-five or thirty shillings. Forty or fifty shillings, I suppose, if he bought it in tots. But we will assume that friend Smith, not yet being case-hardened, has been spending, only about ten shillings a day on his favourite poison. I should be interested to know where the money comes from."

Mrs. Vallence laughed.

"Now don't talk like that and get yourself accused of being an old busybody."

"My dear! When my gardener can suddenly afford to give up work and start poisoning himself with gin I am surely permitted to be a little curious—both as his employer and his vicar. Moreover, I am compelled to hear willy-nilly what the village is saying. I was wondering if he had won a prize in one of those Irish sweepstakes and said nothing about it."

"They've been stopped, haven't they?" Roger said. "At least, so far as this country is concerned. You may | give your money to a bookmaker, but not to a hospital.

Not even an English hospital. You may ruin yourself I by sending ready-money bets to Scotland, or personally distributing it on the racecourse, but that is different. And the legislators themselves can't tell us why."

"They blame us for it, I believe," said Vallence. "The clergy, I mean. And yet Stillby kindly turns his blind eye on the wicked games of chance we have at our garden fete in aid of the church. Er—talking of Stillby, I wonder if Dr. Garrow was able to help him yesterday."

Roger laughed uneasily.

"I shouldn't think so. I was present at the interview. It wouldn't have helped me if I'd been in Stillby's place. The late Mr. Thurley seems to have been as mad as a hatter."

"We-ell, I shouldn't quite say that."

"The secret which he mentioned to you and said would be buried with him—that came out. Or rather the nature of it. Dr. Garrow knew and told Stillby. Thurley claimed to be an alchemist."

"What!" It was Vallence's exclamation, and there was a general laugh. "Dr. Garrow must have invented that tale. Anyhow, how could he know? He was hardly on speaking terms with Thurley."

"So he said. But apparently he'd met Thurley before. Anyhow, he claimed to know what Thurley was working on—and it was that."

"But why should anybody steal the man's body? It reminds, me—I don't wish to make a joke of it, but it reminds me of the goose that laid the golden eggs. Unless—oh, of, course! Unless he expected to find the— er—magic formula in the coffin. Good heavens! I thought we'd only gone back to the days of the body- snatchers, but we seem to have returned to the Dark Ages. The bearded magician in the sugar-loaf hat, abacadabra, love philtres, and all that sort of thing.
Er— surely Dr. Garrow didn't suggest that he himself believed —er—?"

He paused, eyeing Roger curiously, and Roger smiled. "Oh, no, of course not. He just said that Thurley was mad and gave that as his reason for saying it. But you, Mr. Vallence, you believe in—er—"

He paused awkwardly with an apologetic laugh and Mrs. Vallence spoke.

"My husband believes in the Powers of Darkness," she said. "We all do. And we believe that they may be invoked. But poor Mr. Thurley was quite a good man. Eccentric, of course, but we never heard a word against him."

A gleam of humour lit up Roger's face.

"Were the mediaeval alchemists good-living men?" he asked.

Vallence caught the gleam and his own eyes twinkled.

"I believe so. At least the grace was given them to stumble upon a number of genuine scientific discoveries. They couldn't hit the pigeon because it wasn't there, but they sometimes brought down the crow by accident. Just as those who pretended to make love philtres probably lit on some excellent homely remedies for common ailments."

Roger laughed again.

"Can't you imagine the love-lorn girl going to the Wise Woman and saying: 'Thank you for the mixture as before. He doesn't love me yet but all me warts is gone'?"

Sudden laughter from Marjory and both her parents cleared the air. It seemed to Roger that laughter was needed then. And while it lingered another thought—in which there was comfort of a kind, or at least a measure of self-congratulation—flitted across Roger's mind.

They had not asked him if he still had the crucifix.

He did not like prevarication. Still less would he have cared to tell the truth.

CHAPTER XII
THE MAN WITH TOO MUCH MONEY

"Thank you, Trode," said Roger, careful to speak, while the man's gaze was upon his face. Trode lowered his white face an inch or two in acknowledgment as Roger took coffee and biscuits from the tray. Unasked, the deaf-mute had formed the habit of bringing this refreshment to the library every morning at about eleven o'clock. Roger, as usual, broke off work and lit a cigarette.

The door closed softly and Roger, sitting, watched the smoke of his cigarette rise and melt. A calendar in an oak frame, altered by somebody—presumably Trode— from day to day, faced him from the middle of a table and became suddenly a mute reminder. Had he been a member of that strange household for sixteen days? Well, the calendar said so, and no doubt the calendar was right.

He could look back on those days, and now on the present arisen from them, as into a kaleidoscope of swiftly changing emotions. He had worked fairly hard and seemed to have done so little, and this was humiliating. On the other hand, Dr. Garrow did not seem to mind how he was progressing, and that—if in one sense a little disappointing—at least spared him the necessity of making excuses which might have seemed a tacit confession of inefficiency. He was now acclimatised, arid certain vague and almost formless suspicions were lulled. He did not like Dr. Garrow, and felt that he never would, but some of his distrust of the man had vanished.

Strangely, too, he had seen comparatively little of his employer. On most evenings Garrow appeared for dinner in his absurd but still impressive robe. Occasionally he joined Roger at lunch, and at uncertain and therefore unexpected times for a quarter of an hour. Probably he had looked in on several occasions when Roger was out, but He never passed a comment nor asked a question.

It was as if his pleasure were that Roger should do exactly as he liked and go and come as he pleased; and if that were so Roger, while giving his full measure of work, was disposed to gratify him.

This morning Roger, conscientiously aware of having begun work early, and knowing that he could work late if he, wished, considered taking a stroll down into the village. He would soon be short of tobacco, and at that hour there was always the chance of meeting one of the Vallences. Probably and preferably it would be Marjory. He had been to tea at the Vicarage on the previous day, and although he was always welcome—and almost more than welcome—to come every afternoon he had the normal man's dislike to take full advantage of a general invitation.

Marjory had been in his thoughts a great deal during the past fortnight. He was aware that she had very little business to be there. Unmanneredly he had bundled her out, and minx-like she had returned. He was in no position to think of marriage. His present employment was only temporary, and when it was done a large note of interrogation, looming now on his mental horizon, would draw uncomfortably near.

He knew that he would be very foolish to fall in love and, perhaps for that very reason, this was just what he had started to do. It was Love, not Tobacco, which called him down into the village that morning—but he preferred to call it Tobacco.

It ended, of course, in his going downstairs, picking up his hat and stick, and walking out. Having turned from the gates by the empty lodge he had covered a hundred yards or so in the direction of the village when his attention was idly drawn to a man approaching him. Roger knew most of the small local community by sight, and at first he thought that the man approaching him was a stranger. A moment later he was not quite sure. There was something vaguely familiar, or at least reminiscent in the face under the brown trilby hat.

The man was on the youthful side of middle age and neatly dressed in a grey lounge suit. Without hearing him speak it would have been a little difficult to guess his station in life. He looked, thought Roger, as if he had strayed, at least geographically, from his normal existence. A commercial traveller, perhaps, who had somehow got himself lost in the heart of the country.

Roger had given up the idle game of guessing and would have passed on without further thought if the stranger had not smiled apologetically and stopped him.

"Oblige me with a light, please?"

Roger heard the jerky, provincial accent, but he was more concerned with the man's face. He looked at him closely while he struck a match and held it to the cigarette'.

"Thanks. Thanks." The man gave a little bird-like lift to his head. "Beg pardon, sir—you haven't seen anything of my brother?"

Roger thought at first, that he must have been mistaken for someone else.

"I don't know him, do I? And I don't think I've seen you before—although you remind me of somebody."

"My brother, sir, he was down this way about a fortnight ago. Seafaring man."

Instantly Roger's memory went back to the begging sailor in the drive on the day of his arrival. This man's hair was sandy, not red like the sailor's, but the family likeness was stamped upon his face.

"Jittings, sir. Herbert Jittings."

"Had he red hair?" Roger inquired.

The other's face brightened.

"That's him, sir. Can you tell me about him?"

"I don't quite follow you. About a fortnight ago—or just over—a sailor stopped me and tried to touch me. I gave him sixpence, I think. He said he'd lost his money at some pony races and that he'd got a registered letter waiting for him at Reading."

The sandy haired man showed symptoms of excitement.

"That's him, sir—that's him. And I'm his brother. And he hasn't been home yet. And my old Dad and Mother are worried. In fact we're all worried."

Roger nodded sympathetically and made an obvious suggestion.

"Well, I daresay that finding he was broke he went off back to sea again."

"That's what the police chinks—but oe don't. You see, knowing—or rather hoping—the money would be waiting for him at Reading, and him being so close, he'd have gone on to get it. But he didn't. I called in at Reading post office yesterday and there was my own letter addressed to him, still waiting."

Roger's interest began to be sharpened.

"That's certainly odd. Was he seen anywhere after he left here?"

"Yes, sir—at Brocking."

"Let's see, where's that?"

"About three miles up the road *on* the way to Reading from here. He was seen there in the evening. I expect he must have walked on there from here. Looks as if he meant to go to Reading. He had a drink or two in the pub at Brocking—he must have got hold of a bit of money by then, but he couldn't have had much—and left quite sober just before closing time."
The man paused as if for breath.

"There's no news of him on the other side of Brocking, going towards Reading; so it looks as if he must have turned about and come down this way again."

"Well," said Roger, "that's probably what he did. Changed his mind and thought he'd go back to sea."

The missing man's brother shook his head.

"That's what the Police think, but they don't know Herbert. At least, the Police in *these* parts don't know him. He'd got a bit of pay to come in and he was looking forward to a nice rest at home. I was wondering if he'd seen some girl down here. But then he'd have let us know. And certain he'd have gone to Reading to get his money. But he's just vanished—fair vanished."

Roger was sympathetic on the surface, but inwardly he had no misgivings for his seafaring acquaintance of the begged sixpence.

"Oh, he'll turn up—if the Police have promised to help."

The other looked askance, making a long face.

"Well, I don't know. I don't know as the Police will trouble much. They'll think he's gone back to Portsmouth or Southampton and signed on again under any old name. Nobody takes count of missing sailors. They're always here to-day and gone to-morrow. But Pm sure he couldn't have gone back to sea. Not while there was money waiting for him at Reading, and more money due to him through the Board of Trade."

Something in the urgency of the man's manner touched Roger.

"I wish I could help you," he said, "but I don't see how. You seem to be worried about something that you haven't told me, and I have no right to ask."

"You're right, sir." The show of sympathy loosened Jittings's tongue. "It's like this. Herbert's a bit wild. He always was. And we're always worried about him except when he's at home, or we know he's safe at sea. Nobody could ever do much with him. When he was a boy our father gave him a good chance and sent him to the Grammar School. When he'd been there a fortnight the headmaster came and had a long talk with father, and Herbert didn't go to the Grammar School no more. He's never been in trouble—not real trouble—but, you see, we never know with him. You see, sir, we're a respectable family."

Roger understood, reading plainly the thought which haunted the other man's eyes. Crime, Police, Prison, Family Disgrace—it could be summed up in just those words.

"Well," he said cheerfully, "no doubt you'll soon have news of him. If he should happen to come back here and I see him, I'll tell him about your anxiety. And if you care to give me your address I'll drop you a line."

The worried face brightened a little.

"Thank you very much indeed, sir. It's very kind of you."

"Not at all," said Roger. "Good morning."

He passed on. A few minutes later he encountered Marjory, a shopping basket on her arm.

"Hullo!" he said. "I wondered if I were going to see you. Busy this morning?"

"One other call," she answered smiling, "and then I'm finished. No, don't grab my basket. I hate to see a man loaded with shopping."

"Oh, very well" He made a sudden change of tone. "This is a pleasant part of the world I've allowed myself to drift to!"

She gave him a quick, suspicious glance.

"What's the matter now?"

He told her briefly and concluded:

"There you are, Marjory! So this is Dravington! First of all, somebody steals a dead man out of a grave, and now somebody seems to have got away with a live sailor."

Marjory did not smile. She stood looking down long and askance until suddenly she brought her gaze to meet his.

"Do you think," she said, "that there's any connection between the two?"

The words seemed to startle him a little, touching some thought, dormant or yet in embryo, giving him the slight shock which was expressed in a little start and jerk of the head. "Now I wonder what on earth made you say that?" he asked.

Her only answer was that she did not know, and he pressed her no further. He only knew that something had started the same hare in his own mind. The cause, he thought, had nothing to do with telepathy. When strange but apparently unconnected events happen close upon one another it is in human nature to seek links between them.

Roger walked with Marjory as far as the Vicarage, but left her at the gate and began to retrace his steps. His way took him past the modest hostelry which dignified itself with the title of the Dravington Arms Hotel.

He had not previously entered the inn. Generally he passed during those hours when it was closed, and all the excisable refreshment which he required was to be had at Dr. Garrow's, costing him nothing. Possibly the reason for the inn sign is not merely to denote the nature of the house, but to remind or suggest to the passer by that he is thirsty.

If this be so it fulfilled its secondary function in the present instance. Roger walked into the saloon bar and stood alone for nearly a minute until the landlady came up to serve him. This partial neglect, he was aware, was due to a disturbance which had been going on in the public bar. It seemed that she had been standing by her husband who, as Roger entered, was ushering a man into the street. Roger heard the final injunction.

"Now you get off home. And don't you come here again until you're sober."

The landlord's wife came up to the counter with a frown which lingered on her face while she took Roger's order.

"Glass of bitter, sir? Yes, sir."

"Bit of trouble here?" said Roger. "Rather unusual at this hour in the morning, isn't it?"

"Yes," she said briefly and resentfully.

The ejected one moved from the door no further than to the edge of the pavement where he stood with drooping knees in evident indecision. Roger could see him through an opening in one of the frosted glass windows. He was a middle-aged, shabby fellow, weather-beaten and slightly bald. Roger, watching him stand there fuddled, wondered idly what he would do next and how long he would take in doing it. A voice from outside put a sudden closure on speculation, and startled Roger no less than the delinquent. For the voice was Dr. Garrow's.

"Smith! Here, Smith!"

It seemed to Roger that the man made an instant effort to pull himself together and that he partly succeeded. He turned his head with an "Oh, 'ullo, sir!" which sounded almost apologetic.

"What are you doing—like this? Why aren't you at work?"

"I'm sorry, sir. I didn't feel none too well, and took a day off."

"Well, I can't have this. Look at me and listen. You mustn't drink!"

"I'm all right, sir."

"You're not. But you've the sense to understand me. You know why you mustn't drink. If you do—well!"

There was a wealth of warning in that last word which no doubt was accompanied by a shrug.

" 'S'll right, sir. I knows what I'm doing. I'm all right. I got control *here.*"

There must have been an accompanying gesture which- Roger did not see. Then Dr. Garrow's voice sounded again.

"So you say. Now I'm giving you a warning. You don't want to make an enemy of me, do you?"
Again there was that note of menace, and this time it had its full effect. The little outburst of only three words was dramatic by reason of the sudden terror in the voice that uttered them.

"God forbid, sir!"

"Get straight home, then, and sleep it off."

That ended the interview and Roger, suddenly concerned with a newly kindled thought, scarcely heard the final injunction? He was wondering if Dr. Garrow had seen him enter and, in that event, if Dr. Garrow would object. It was unlikely that Garrow would walk inside, but there was the possibility. And for no reason that he could have given he did not welcome the thought of meeting and talking with him just then.

The possibility, however, remained only for a moment. Dr. Garrow walked on, and Roger saw the broad of his back after he had-passed the opening in the windows. He turned with a breath of relief and saw that the landlord had now come up to the counter. The landlord was grinning and he winked.

"That was Dr. Garrow seeing him off, sir. Funny, that. You'd think he was Dr. Garow's own man and not the Vicar's."

"The Vicar's?"

"Yes, sir. Nice thing if Mr. Vallence was to get to hear of this—but don't you tell'him, sir. I knows you know Mr. Vallence. At least I've seen you talk to Miss Vallence. Just come to live down this way, sir?"

"Well, for the time," said Roger.

He had his wits about him. It seemed that the landlord, evidently curious as he was, did not yet know that he was in Dr. Garrow's employ. On the other hand, Roger, as a friend of the Vicar's family, was a person deserving a measure of respect.

"I was wondering if you was a detective at first, sir."

"What! Oh—about that missing body case? No, not guilty."

The landlord grinned although his curiosity was yet unassuaged.

"We've had a lot of strangers down here lately over that. Detectives and newspaper men. Well, it ain't done us no harm. But there's always trouble where there's good luck, and I don't want to risk my licence over a man like Smith. He was well on the way last night, sir; and then he took three large bottles of Old 'ome with him.' Must have had those this morning before he came down. Looked to me like it when he first came in."

Roger laughed tolerantly.

"He's the Vicar's gardener, isn't he? Yes, I rather gathered that he'd been taking a holiday for some days. Well, boys will be boys."

The landlord grinned again.

"That's all very well, sir, but if he ain't careful Mr. Vallence'll never take him back. And o' course everybody's wondering where he got the money. There's a rumour about the Irish Sweep, but I believe all that's been stopped; and besides, it's some while since the Grand National and he'd have had the money weeks ago in any case."

"I should have thought so," said Roger.

"Well, sir, he's not a bad chap in some ways, is Smith, so I'd take it kindly if you didn't tell the Vicar or any of his family what you've just seen. The time will come when the poor chap won't have no money, and if he's got no work where will he be?"

Roger tried to show by his manner as much as by his words that his secrecy in that respect was to be trusted. He gave the required assurance but added: "Still, it's a hundred to one he knows."

The landlord nodded.

"Well, he's a good, broad-minded one for a parson and a proper gentleman. And we've 'ad some queer fish about 'ere—I give you my word. What do you think of that there Thurley—the funny old bloke who died and then his body got dug up and pinched?"

Roger shrugged his shoulders and smiled.

"I don't know what to make of that. I never knew him. It happened, of course, before I came here."

The landlord was smiling, but in his eyes there was just the shadow of the dark wings of fear. There was awe too in the voice which he lowered before he spoke again.

"I know what happened to that joker. If you ask *me,* the devil ran away with him." '

"The devil?" said Roger, smiling.

"Yes, sir, the devil. But that's not the name he's known by round here. It begins with a G—and he calls himself a doctor."

There was' a pause. Roger's eyes narrowed suddenly as they met the half sheepish gaze of the man beyond the counter. He was surprised almost as Marjory had surprised him less than an hour ago; but now anger was mixed with the other emotion—an anger directed inwardly upon himself but showing on his face and in the tone in which he spoke.

"Look here," he began coldly and gruffly, and then paused. "Look here, you know, you've no right to say that. I'm sorry. This is partly my fault. I ought perhaps to have told you who I was. You would have understood then that I'm the last person you should say that to. I am employed by Dr. Garrow. I am his secretary and librarian."

The landlord jerked up a face which looked as if it had been suddenly slapped. There was genuine fear now in the eyes which flinched before Roger's gaze.

"Good Lord! I beg your pardon, sir. I didn't know. Really I didn't know."

"That's all right. But you understand my position, don't you?"

"What, sir?"

"I can't listen to idle talk about him." Conscience nudged him here. "That is to say—"

"No, sir. Certainly not, sir. Here, sir, have a drink with me, sir. Just to show there's no ill-feeling."

"That's all right," said Roger, laughing. "There isn't any."

"Sure, sir?" The man's manner was ingratiating and very urgent. "Then, sir, you won't tell him what I said? Promise, sir? Promise?"

CHAPTER XIII
SUDDEN DEATH

Roger did not see Dr. Garrow at lunch time that day, and did not know if he were in or out. He never questioned Trode concerning his master's movements; for this would have entailed putting pencil to paper, thus turning seemingly casual inquiry into overt curiosity.

Sometimes he wrote Trode a brief note asking what he thought might be Dr. Garrow's wishes in small, unforeseen circumstances, or bidding Trode inquire; but that was as far as he went.
After his solitary meal he went upstairs to the library and continued his work. The ink-well needed refilling, and after a while he went to a cupboard where ink was kept in a large stone bottle.

It was while he was removing the bottle that he saw something in the cupboard which he had not noticed before. This was a ball apparently of clear, colourless glass, mounted on a little silver stand.

Roger knew what it was at a glance. He had seen one, and only one, before. It belonged to one of his aunts who imagined herself to possess—as she called them—"psychic gifts." The good lady was a dreamer and interpreter of dreams, and after an important event she had always her tale of the dream which foretold it. To such a woman a crystal was almost a necessity; and here in the cupboard was one—almost a replica in size and with the little pedestal on which it stood—of that which Aunt Imogen had once shown him.

Idly he looked into its depths and saw, apparently in its centre, a little white focus of light.-That, he knew, was the spot one was supposed to watch while waiting for the marvels to be revealed.

Self-hypnotism, of course, he thought; and he remembered idling at school on an occasion after he had finished Prep, and trying—not quite without success—to see pictures in the ink-well. It occurred to him just then that if he were a man with a highly developed imagination he ought to see a vision of Marjory.

Now that he was caught thinking of her the idle moment lengthened. The time was inopportune, for he succeeded in fixing his attention to an extent which precluded his hearing the rattle of the door-knob. At a sound which followed immediately he turned with a slight start and looked behind him. But already he had been detected. The open doorway framed Dr. Garrow.

"Hullo," said Garrow softly and pleasantly. "Ah, you found that somewhere about, did you? I have another and a larger one in my room. Have you seen anything at all—interesting?"

Roger tried hard to hide confusion, but it refused quite to be hidden and looked out through a slightly heightened colour. He laughed.

"Oh, I've just come across it," he said, "and I was wondering how people managed to persuade themselves that they saw things. Real pictures, I mean; not merely lights."

He was about to continue and try to cover his retreat with some facetious remark, but an inner monitor warned him that this might not be wise. It would be at least as well to put a plain question first.

"Do you believe in this sort of thing?" he inquired casually.

Dr. Garrow smiled and came over to him.

"What do you mean by 'this sort of thing'?" he asked. "Shall I see a horse passing the post in a race timed for to-morrow or next week? I doubt it. Do you see anything?"

"I can see my own reflection when I put my head in the shadow of the curtain."

"Hardly enough to make crystal-gazing popular," said Dr. Garrow with a gentle laugh. "Look again for a few seconds."

He dropped a hand lightly and, it seemed, playfully on .Roger's shoulder. Roger looked and found the globe shadowed so that his own face looked back. Then a sharp ejaculation came from him.

That face, looking upwards as if mirrored in a pool—that long, sad, beautiful face, suffering yet infinitely evil —was surely never his own. He felt his heart plunge like a kicking horse, and the start lifted his gaze. In an instant he was aware that the hand resting upon his shoulder had felt the reverberation.

"Why! Hullo!" Dr. Garrow's voice, and the laugh which followed upon the words, were charged with a gentle banter. "Did we fancy that we saw something?"

"I saw my own reflection," said Roger, laughing and looking round. He had—or thought he had—got the reins of himself again.

"My dear fellow, you mustn't tell people that. I mean you mustn't own to the little shock it gave you. It would give the impertinent and would-be witty too great an opportunity. 'Think,' they might say, 'how we are compelled to suffer!"'

He made one of his sudden changes of tone.

"Of course, there is nothing in it—except what one imagines. I shouldn't look again."

"I don't suppose I shall. And no reasonable person— I mean I never imagined there was anything in it. Yet —well, I suppose I had better not say it."

Dr. Garow laughed in high good humour.

"Well," he said, "and suppose I say that you had better out with it—whatever it was."

"You say there's nothing in it. Yet this belongs to you. And you tell me you have another."

"Ah, I am by nature an experimentalist. I scout nothing until I have tested it. Besides, I didn't quite say that there was nothing in it. I said there was nothing in it for you."

Roger seized upon that last accentuated word.

"For anyone?" he asked.

"There will shortly be prizes at Olympia—is it Olympia nowadays?—for throwing the hammer, lifting weights, running certain distances, and so forth. But they certainly won't be for me, and probably not for you. There is such a thing as training."

"Then you say there is something in—er—this for certain people?"

"I said nothing of the sort," said Dr. Garrow lightly, 'and you are not to put words into my mouth."

It was like the man. He had the advantages of his age and his relative position. He could dangle the thread to the kitten and snatch it away as he chose. If the kitten caught the thread he could let go and abandon the game. Roger had the intuition to see that Garrow would hardly be worsted in an argument, and certainly never by any person in his employ.

"And now," said the Doctor, with another -sudden change of manner and tone, "tell me what you've been doing to-day."

"Do you mean here?"

"No, no. You're making good progress. I can see that without being told. You were out this morning. Did anything of any—er—interest come your way?"

"No-o," Roger began, and checked himself. "Oh!"

"Yes?"

"Day I arrived here—before I got to the house—I met a sailor coming down the drive. He was a red-headed fellow, begging. Wanted to get home somewhere in the Midlands. You'd helped him a little, I think."

"Yes, I remember. Well?"

"His brother was in the village looking for him."

Dr. Garrow was frowning, but he smiled.

"I remember the man you mean. Yes, I was rather weak and gave him something. But he told me he hadn't any home or any relatives. Well, didn't he get home?"

"Apparently not. Got to some place a mile or two beyond here and then vanished. No trace of him at all." Dr. Garrow seemed only mildly interested.

"It's a way sailors have," he said lightly. "And nearly always they reappear. Take the classic instance Of Jonah. Who, observing his plight at the time, would have expected to see him again? Yet, having proved an emetic for whales, he made triumphant return and became a prophet. There's no saying where a sailor will go, or where he'll afterwards tell you he's been."
And Dr. Garrow laughed almost silently, but with evident enjoyment of his own 'not too brilliant pleasantry. Then he hesitated, backed a step and turned. "I shall see you at dinner," he said.
He went out swiftly and quietly. Roger stared at the closing door, amazed at something which was happening in his inner consciousness. It was as if the spirit, acting independently of the brain, had uttered a slow, prolonged, almost inaudible sigh of relief.

For no clear reason that he could have expressed even to his own questioning self, Roger did not look forward to meeting Dr. Garrow at dinner that night. But Garrow's manner dispelled that subtle, unpleasant impression which he had left on Roger in the library.

If he had known of that impression and set himself to remove it he could hardly have made a more effective and less obvious effort. He set the conversational pace and talked lightly of current affairs, jumping from sport—of which he seemed to have at least an average knowledge—to books, and from books to the international situation.

-When Trode brought in the coffee Garrow looked closely at him and began to talk rapidly on his fingers. Trode made shorter replies after the same fashion and presently went out. When he had gone, Garrow turned to Roger with a deprecatory smile.

"Did you see how Trode was looking?" he asked. "Well—no," Roger answered. "I didn't notice particularly. He always looks rather ill to me."

Garrow's brows rose quickly and fell above a swift, meaning glance.

"Ah," he said, "you don't yet know the signs. There may be squalls tonight. You remember once before?"

"You mean that he'll have a nightmare and start screaming?"

"Well, he looks as if something of that sort may be coming on. I've packed him off to bed now."
"I should have thought that this would have been the time to keep him up."

"Not in the least. If I've got to go and pacify him, I'd sooner that it happened at midnight than at two or three in the morning. Anyhow, I shall give him until midnight before I turn in. Would you care for a game of chess upstairs?"

"Certainly, if you like; but I can't give you much of a game."

"You can, if you like to help me with a couple of problems. They have just occurred to me. They both look like inevitable mates, and you shall be the attacking force. I want to see if there is any way of wriggling out."

They went up to the library and got out the board and the chessmen. At the end of an hour Garrow suddenly started up.

"Aha," he said, "did you hear that?"

Roger was silent, listening. Garrow rose, went to the door and without another word stole softly out. Roger remained sitting still, while the door stayed open.

He waited, straining his ears, beset once more by a sense of eeriness, and suddenly started and then grimaced with annoyance. The involuntary start he had given came from so small a cause as the clock behind him beginning to chime the hour of ten. He looked at his watch, to find that it was set right within a few seconds, and his gaze was still upon the dial when he heard Garrow's voice in a distant part of the house.

He could not hear what Garrow said, and the muffled reverberations soon faded into silence. After a few minutes Garrow returned smiling.

"All is well now," he remarked. "I have laid the ghost. In other words, I don't think friend Trode will ride the nightmare any more this evening. It was your move, I think?"

Half an hour later Garrow yawned, smiled and then apologised.

"Yes," he added, "There's no denying what that means. I don't know how you feel—about turning in."

"Just as you like," said Roger. "I can't generally sleep."

They parted a few minutes later. Within half an hour Roger had fulfilled his own expectation; and Trode awoke him on the morrow with tea at the usual hour.

The fine weather had broken for the time being, and clouds moving from the West were dropping fine rain when Roger set out for his morning stroll. A few yards from the outskirts of the village a stile on the right hand gave access to a footpath, which Roger now noticed for the first time. He now noticed it only because his attention was drawn in that direction by the sight of two blue helmets bobbing above the level of the hedge. A moment or two later the aperture, as he drew level with it, brought two policemen into full view.

Evidently they had been bending over the ground, but they stood upright as Roger's footfalls approached and remained staring at him as he passed.

They said nothing, but allowed a cold, detached, almost truculent air to speak for them. "Now just you pass on and mind your own business"—that, thought Roger smiling, was what they meant and what they would have said.

A car was approaching from behind him, and with a hand concealed from the two officers he made a warning gesture; but the driver had already seen the approach to the village and was dropping to a decorous, law-abiding speed.

Roger, with no thought other than that he had passed a trap for motorists, went on into the village and saw a crowd of loiterers about the outside of the Dravington Arms. They had the subdued air of people waiting for a funeral, and Roger, pausing beside a man whose gaze was on the stable gate, turned to inquire.

"What's everybody waiting for?"

"Ambulance," the man answered simply. "The body's down the yard."

"The body? What body?"

The other looked mildly surprised.

"Haven't you heard, sir?"

"No. What?"

"Well, it's suicide I should think. Some say it ain't."

"Oh, you mean somebody dead. Who—?"

"Man named Smith, sir. Found dead last night. He'd been on the drink for some time and I think he done his- self in. But nobody's got the rights of it yet."

"Not Smith the Vicar's gardener?"

"Well, he was—up to a short while ago. That's the man, sir. Ah, here comes the Red Cross van."

In the general buzz of excitement Roger turned to his informant again.

"I saw some policemen up the road," he said, "just inside the hedge by the footpath—"

"Ay, that's right. That's where the body was found. Smith must have been on his way home. They're keeping people back until the ground's been properly examined for footprints and all that, I s'pose."

The van halted. The policeman alighted and hurried down the yard, the foremost shouldering a folded stretcher. After a brief interval they reappeared, carrying the stretcher between them. Something lay upon it, hidden by a blanket, and some of the sightseers doffed their hats.

The stretcher and its hidden burden vanished inside the van. The engine started and the van slowly wheeled, forcing a passage for itself, and drove off in the direction of the mortuary. The gaze of the almost silent cluster of people followed it up the road.

Roger turned and went on.

CHAPTER XIV
THE INSPECTOR WANTS TO KNOW

Marjory, whom Roger had half expected to see, was not in sight when he reached the outside of the post office. But his disappointment was short-lived, for when he entered to buy some stamps he saw her standing at the counter.

The woman on the other side was talking volubly in a hushed voice which sank still lower as Roger made his presence known.

Marjory turned towards him at once with a little exclamation of greeting and a sudden smile on a face which lacked its usual colour.

"Hullo!" She paused and lowered her voice. "I'm so glad you happened to come along. I'll wait for you outside."

"Well, I only want to get some stamps. I shan't be—"

"I'll wait for you outside," Marjory repeated. Obviously she wanted to escape from the woman behind the counter. Roger understood and smiled. As Marjory withdrew he turned and asked for a two shilling book of stamps.

"Terrible thing!" groaned the woman, eyeing her next potential victim.

"On the contrary. It's the most convenient way of buying stamps."

"I mean, about the murder, sir."

"Yes, I've just been hearing about it. A book of stamps, please."

"Poor Smith! He was in here only yesterday morning. Quite early—but he'd had one or two already, if you know what I mean. I don't know who murdered him, and I'm sure I wish I did, but I've got my own ideas about how it came to happen. *Somebody's* been talking too much!"

"I shouldn't wonder," said Roger, with a kind of good- humoured impatience. "A book—"

"Yes, sir. Have they taken the body to the mortuary yet, do you know? I've been peeping out through the window, but people keep on coming in and talking to me so that I haven't had the chance to keep Oh Fie with what's going on."

"They've just taken the body away, and I want—"

"I haven't a book left, sir, so will you take sixteen three-halfpennies, or twelve penny and twelve half—Oh, no, that wouldn't be right. What would that come to? What with murders—"

"Twenty-four'pennies and twelve halfpennies will do."

"Thank you, sir. I suppose you didn't actually *see* the body going out. Oh, no, they'd have had it covered up with something, I'm sure. A blanket, I expect, although who'd want the blanket again afterwards? I know a man—Once borrowed a pair of my late husband's trousers and committed suicide in them when they was nearly new. That was years ago. Well, my husband was a bit particular and he didn't fancy wearing those trousers again. So what do you think happened?"

Roger sighed and said that he didn't know. The stamps meanwhile were being slowly torn from the sheet.

"He gives them to the Vicar for a jumble sale. And his Aunt Aggie—my husband's aunt, I mean—goes to the jumble sale and sees them same trousers. 'Why,' she says, 'they'll just fit Bert'—that was my husband's name —'and dirt cheap at three and six.' So Bert gets his own trousers back almost as soon as he got rid of them. So what do you think he done then?"

Roger's fingers were reaching under the steel wire of the protecting cage. The question was not one for him to answer, and the woman proceeded to tell him as slowly she surrendered his purchase.

"He wore them trousers for the rest of his life. No, I don't really mean that, of course, but just for so long as they lasted out. Because he said he could see the workings of Providence and it was a lesson to him not to be fussy about little things. 'Ah' he used to say, 'there's more in these trousers than meets the eye.' He could make that tale last out a good hour and a half, for he was always a free-spoken man. And people used to ask him why he didn't go a bit more by me and learn that silence is sometimes golden."

Roger at last seized the stamps and hurried out. He joined Marjory a few yards away.

"Sorry," he said briefly.

"I know," she answered without smiling. "She's awful. And—isn't it a terrible thing? About poor Smith, I mean. Can you spare any time this morning?"

"Of course. Why?"

"Then will you come home for a few minutes? Inspector Stillby's there and wants to see you."

"Inspector Stillby? Wants to see *me?*

"Yes. As I went out I told Father I thought I might be seeing you. And the Inspector, who was with him at the time, said he'd like to speak to you. And—well, Father thought it might be more convenient if you came up to the Vicarage and saw him there."

Roger passed a hand over his brow.

"Oh, thanks. Yes. But what on earth does he think I can tell him? I didn't leave the house yesterday evening.

"No. I said I didn't think you did. But the Inspector said that if you *had* happened to go out you'd have had to pass the scene of—you know. And I think he wanted to know if you saw any strangers loitering near there or—you know—anything that can provide him with a clue."

Roger shrugged his shoulders.

"Why should he fasten on me? But I'd better come up and see him or else he'll be ferreting me out at Dr. Garrow's place. I say—this is pretty awful for you. You knew Smith so well."

"Yes, we—I—can't realize it yet."

They went together to the Vicarage. Marjory left him at the door of her father's study and Roger went in to exchange greetings with him. The Inspector stood in the background for half a minute while they talked. Then Vallence motioned him across.

"Sit down, Roger. Do take a chair, Inspector. Roger, the Inspector wants to know—"

"Allow me, sir," the Inspector interrupted.

He turned to Roger who was in the act of sitting down.

"Good morning, sir. We've met before, if you remember. You were good enough to procure me an interview with Dr. Garrow. You know, of course, what brings me here. I'll cut it as short as I can."

He paused and coughed.

"About the deceased—the man Smith. You know the spot where the body was found?"

"Roughly, I think, yes. Just by the footpath on the other side of the stile going—"

"That's it. And we know when the crime must have taken place to within a very few minutes. Now, sir, I think you was seen passin' close by that spot within that period of time. Not goin' by the footpath, I mean, but straight along the road."

Roger smiled and shook his head.

"Your information is wrong," he said. "I didn't leave Dr. Garrow's house yesterday evening."

"Ah!" said Inspector Stillby. "Ah, that's a pity. Because I hoped you would be able to help me. Now, excuse me, sir, thiirk again. Think hard. What were you doing at ten o'clock last night?"

"I can tell you exactly. I was in Dr. Garrow's library. And I am quite sure of the time because of a small incident. Oh, by the way, here is my watch set by the library clock. I haven't had occasion to alter it since."

"Thank you. Now do you mind telling me what makes you sure that you were in the library at ten o'clock."

"Certainly. The Doctor's man. Trode, wasn't looking very well when he served dinner. He always does look pretty ghastly, but Dr. Garrow seemed to think he was looking worse than usual and sent him to bed. Besides being a deaf-mute, he's a bit mental, I believe. He walks in his sleep and wakes up and screams, and Dr. Garrow has to go to him. I'd had one experience of that."

"Ah?" said the Inspector, nodding.

"Well, Dr. Garrow and I sat down and played chess, and after a while Dr. Garrow heard Trode yell out and went off to quieten him."

"Did you hear him call out when Dr. Garrow heard him?"

"I? No. I'm not sure. I can't say for certain."

"I see. Thank you. Go on."

"Dr. Garrow went off and I heard his voice in the distance talking to the man."

The Inspector's eyes narrowed.

"Talking to a deaf man, Mr. Moorlock?"

Roger, slightly annoyed, felt his colour rising.

"Oh, I think one does that involuntarily. I often speak to Trode. Besides, he understands lip-reading to some extent."

"Not in the dark, surely?"

"I am not at all sure that they n>ere in the dark. I didn't see them. I can only tell you what I heard, and that makes me so sure of the time. While Dr. Garrow was still out of the room the clock chimed ten. My watch was right by it then and it's still almost right. That's how I know exactly where I was at ten o'clock, and I know Dr. Garrow can bear me out."

The Inspector smiled.

"That's all right, Mr. Moorlock. So you can't have been the mysterious stranger seen close to the spot within a few minutes of the crime. If you had been, your passing along the road would have been in the natural order of things and of no use to us as a clue— unless you could have told us of something that you had seen or heard. Well, we must look elsewhere. I will wish both you gentlemen good morning."

The Vicar saw his official visitor to the door and came back at once to Roger. He was smiling.

"My dear fellow," he said, "I am so sorry. That fool of a man asking you all those questions and trying to catch you tripping. I can't think how on earth the police go about their work. Now suppose you had been near the place at the time of the crime and noticed anything suspicious you'd only have been too glad to help the police."

"Naturally."

There was a. silence, broken at last by a sudden exclamation from Vallence.

"Good heavens!" he said softly. "I've suddenly seen it."

Roger, slightly startled by the change in the Vicar's manner, looked up sharply.

'Yes?" he said. "Seen what, Mr. Vallence?"

"The arch-subtlety of that policeman. He didn't want to know where you were at the time of the murder. *You* didn't come into his reckoning at all. He wanted to know whether Dr. Garrow and his creature Trode were at home. And that was his way of finding out."
Roger drew a long breath.

"Is that what you really think?"

"I'm fairly sure."

"Well, why on earth should Dr. Garrow murder a jobbing gardener?"

"I didn't say that was my suspicion, and I don't suppose it was our friend Stillby's. I think *he* was more interested in Trode. You see, a lot of people around here think that that fellow's mental. But it seems he was having an attack of some sort at the very moment—or near enough to the very moment—of the crime."

Roger pursed X»-s lips as if to whistle.

"Stillby waters run deep," he said.

"Yes," agreed Vallence, and laughed. Then he grew grave again. "But—er—perhaps this isn't a time for joking. Poor Smith, you know. Er—can you manage to stay for lunch?"

Roger hesitated and shook his head in replying.

"No, thanks very much. I don't think I'd better to-day. Must run back and go on with my work. Interview with the police will be my excuse if explanations are required."

At that moment Marjory opened the door, looked in and hesitated.

"May I?" she asked. "I saw the Inspector going. Or are you talking privately, you two?"

"No," said her father, "come along in. I've asked him to stay to lunch. My entreaty has failed;
You may try, my child."

"Sorry," said Roger, "but I've got to earn my bread. Of course, I couldn't help stealing some time off this morning. I'm going to tell him. Ten to one he's missed me in any case. But I'd like to come round this afternoon, if I may. I'll just take the temperature. I don't want him to round on me suddenly and say that I'm not pulling my weight."

CHAPTER XV
ENDING IN A KISS

Dr. Garrow was sitting in the hall when Roger returned. Roger had an idea that his return had been awaited, despite the older man's usual urbanity of manner and his brief smile of welcome. Behind it all there was a subtle suggestion of the office tyrant who had caught the clerk returning over late from lunch.

"Ah," he said, "good morning—or rather good afternoon. A longer stroll than usual?"

"Yes," said Roger; "I'm sorry, but I had to go up to the Vicarage. The police wanted to see me."

Dr. Garrow's eyebrows were raised.

"The police wanted to see you? Why?"

"Somebody alleged to be like me was supposed to have been noticed near the scene of the murder last night."

"The murder!" said Dr. Garrow, in blank astonishment. "What murder?"

"Haven't you heard? The whole neighbourhood—but of course you haven't been out. Smith, the part-time gardener at the Vicarage, has been found killed."

The Doctor said something below his breath. He edged his chair nearer to the spot where Roger was standing.

"You don't mean that! I knew the man. When? Where? Tell me."

"Last night. Round about ten o'clock, they think. Anyhow, the Inspector heard that I passed near the spot and thought I might be able to help him. Or he put it that way. But I was able to assure him that I wasn't there. At least I said that you could tell him that I was in the library at that time. That seemed to satisfy him so far as I was concerned."

Dr. Garrow smiled suddenly.

"Ah, you told him that? I'm very glad. But—give me the details."

"I really don't know them. It seems that he was on his way at about ten last night, and had just got on to a footpath this side of the village—"

"Ah, I know," said Dr. Garrow. "And a stranger like you—for you're still a stranger here to most—had been in the vicinity at the time? Yes, I follow you. Well, you weren't in any grave peril this morning. There couldn't have been any motive to kill the man. Besides, I could certainly swear that you were here. That must have been about the time that Trode had one of his attacks."

"It was," said Roger simply.

"Had he any known enemies? What does the—er— the Vicar think of it?"

"I don't know. But if the man hadn't enemies, he had money. He'd given up work for some time and taken to drink."

"I am aware of that. I saw him—it may have been only yesterday—very much the worse for liquor, and remonstrated with him. So the police think that robbery was the motive? And that suggests some local man— or men—who knew his habits and the fact of his having money. The police have plenty to work on. No doubt we shall hear of his arrest before very long."

He paused and uttered his cricket-like chirrup.

"I was trying to make up my mind," he resumed, "to come and join you at lunch. But I don't think I will. As you know, I eat little during the day. Trode will look after you."

"Thank you," said Roger, and saw Garrow making a move as if for departure. "I am sorry to have wasted so much of the morning."

"My dear fellow, not at all. I am not hurrying you. I have urged you before to take your time."
Garrow seemed in high good humour and Roger seized the opportunity.

"Then you won't mind if I go out again in the afternoon? I can make it up tonight."

"Certainly. Certainly. There are two walks in life by which I could never have marched to success—and they are closely parallel. I cannot imagine myself a captain of industry or a slave-driver. I shall see you at dinner, then?"

Roger was left gratified by his success in dealing with a man who required to be studied. He had never liked Garrow nor ever could like him—those incidents full of abominable suggestion and that infernal tapestry fronting him on the wall were reasons enough—but the man knew how to dispel at least a little of the instinctive aversion he caused in others.

So shortly after three o'clock Roger walked again to the Vicarage. It was Marjory herself who opened the door to him.

"Father's disappeared," she announced.

She laughed next moment at the sight of his face.

"I mean," she said, still laughing and laying a hand on his sleeve, "he's gone out, or hidden himself away because we've just heard- that the Misses Bates are coming over to tea. Or, rather, Mother remembered that she'd asked them. So let's bolt, shall we?"

"I don't quite follow," said Roger. "Who are the Misses Bates?"

"One of them is like the unpleasant old lady in the Old Testament who lived at Endor. And the other one is like the bad fairy who wasn't asked to the christening. Mother says she doesn't mind them. Father says that he feels bound to love all God's creatures, but there are one or two duty calls he ought to pay—and now's the time. So what shall we do?"

Roger laughed.

"It sounds desperate: What do you suggest?"

"I've got my hat on."

"So I see?"

"And there's my mac hanging up."

"Oh, is that yours?"

"Mother wears it sometimes. Well? Oh, Roger, my dear, do wake up. I'm not suggesting that you should take me to Gretna."

"I wish you would. But I don't follow."

She drew back and made him a deep *obeissance.*

"Dear, kind, thick-headed *angel,"* she said, "will you *please* take me out for a walk and give me tea somewhere?"

"Oh, rather," he laughed.

"Come on, then. Let's bolt. I'm sick of talk about stolen bodies and murders and disappearances; and the Misses Bates are only coming to dig all that up again. I don't think it's going to rain to-day."

She was wrong. An hour later they were standing under a tree in a deep cutting, watching the level flight of rain and listening to the level murmur of the drenching leaves. He had slipped his hand inside her arm and talk waned until suddenly she asked him what he was thinking He answered laughing.

"I was thinking how rotten it must have been for old Noah in the ark."

"I see," said Marjory, with studied coldness. She gently disengaged his hand. "With nobody much but Mrs. Noah—"

"A stiffly built and rather wooden sort of person, I always imagined. That's just the point. He hadn't you with him."

Marjory laughed. Her gaze was upon his, for she had not been born in an age of coyness. But she kept it lifted only for a moment.

"That's not at all bad for you, Roger," she said, "but it would have gone a lot better in 1840. Then I should have had to toss my head—I wonder how they managed that—and murmur: 'Oh, really, Mr. Moorlock! I don't know what Mamma would say if she knew you said such things'."

"Then I should say: 'Miss Marjory—may I call you, Marjory?—I think you know my secret.' Your turn next. You say: 'Pray, Mr. Moorlock, I must not hear you. My heart is already given to another'."

"That last bit," said Marjory, "wouldn't be true."

"Or—'You must ask Papa, who will doubtless overlook any moral defects if your bank account is satisfactory'. Then Papa, when consulted, would ask if I knew any actresses. I should then basely conceal the fact that I had once been to the Theatrical Garden Party. He would then examine my pass book, going through it with the air of a chartered accountant looking for defalcations. Then he would hand it back to me with a sigh, remarking: 'Would you mind pulling the bell? I want my boots.' "

She laughed and drew half a pace away from him.

"All the same," she said, "I believe they were happier days. Kissing has got cheap—like everything else. People are too hasty to-day and they've lost their shyness."

"Oh, have they!" said Roger bitterly. "Not all of 'em!"

She disregarded the remark which he ended with a sudden, half, self-deprecatory laugh.

"Do you know what I think?" she said slowly, frowning over her nails. "I think that if I were in love—and sure that He was in love with me—the happiest time would be then, before we ever spoke of it. Or that would be the happiest time to look back upon?"

"Logically, of course, that's absurd."

"I know; but love isn't logical."

"Oh," he laughed, "sending the logicians to keep company with the locksmiths, aren't you? And, anyhow, what do you know about it?"

"Nothing," said Marjory, with sudden colour in her cheeks.

Roger's right arm seemed suddenly to act of its own independent will. It went slowly and gently round Marjory's shoulders. Then, "Damn!" said Roger under his breath, and snatched it away.

Marjory understood on the instant the reason for the anti-climax. Footfalls had suddenly become audible, plodding towards them down the lane. She glanced back in their direction and a young farm-hand came into view, walking with the laboured yet tireless gait of a shire horse at plough.

"It's young Percy Bodding," she said.

The Mr. Bodding who had been endowed with a Christian name which has made a meteoric descent of the social firmament during the past two generations was a short, heavy, clumsy specimen of his kind. Seven years compulsory education—from teachers who remained un-cultured despite their Government certificates—had just enabled him to read a little with difficulty and write a little with agony. However, these small attainments sufficed. He could fill in football coupons—or cowpons, as he preferred to call them—and read for himself on Sunday the brief obituary of a day's wages.

Marjory retired a decorous short step from Roger's side. She was aware that in young Bodding's eyes, when they were turned in Roger's and her direction, there might appear a scene reminiscent to him of rustic courtship. And young Bodding would grin and touch his cap and wish a respectful good afternoon—and afterwards relate a tale in the most disrespectful language, bristling with innuendo. She knew her yokels. She was also suddenly aware that it had stopped raining.

Young Bodding's day's toil was not yet over. He was but passing down the lane from one field to another.

Hence the desultory gait. He looked up and saw her suddenly and grinned as he touched his cap.

Marjory sang out to him in the high, pleasant voice which denies embarrassment.

"Good afternoon, Percy."

"Afternoon, Miss."

The grin embraced Roger and became apologetic as he swerved a little from his direction and came diagonally across the lane. Obviously he had something to say. He began to say it to Marjory, but looked at Roger most of the time.

"Excuse me, Miss. Do you know anybody who's lost something? My mother found it in a 'edge. It's silver, Miss—at least it looks like silver. Like what the Papists worship. And they 'ave them in the 'Igh Church, too. A Cross, you know, Miss, and—"

"Oh, you mean a crucifix?" said Marjory..

"That's right, Miss. Well, my mother, she's got sharp eyes, and she 'appened to see it in a 'edge last evening. Down Warren Lane. Looked as if somebody must have throwed it there."
Roger found the resultant spell of silence highly uncomfortable.

"You had better tell your mother," said Marjory at last, "to bring it to the Vicarage. If we can find the owner we will, and no doubt your mother will get a reward."

"Very good, Miss. She don't want what isn't hers— although it's silver, like, you see. And being something what might be useful to Mr. Vallence—"

Marjory interrupted.

"All right, Percy. You tell her to bring it along and we'll try to find the owner."

"Very good, Miss. Thank you. Good afternoon, Miss. Good afternoon, Sir."

He went shambling on. Roger followed him with his gaze, conscious of a portentous silence beside him.

"Well," said Marjory, suddenly and a little heavily, "have you lost anything?"

He turned uncomfortably.

"Yes. Er—what you gave me. And I suppose that's what he's found. I put it in a drawer in my room and it went. I didn't like to say anything—after what you and your father had told me. I thought it might disturb you."

Her eyes had narrowed and her lips suddenly tightened.

"Doesn't that prove anything to you?"

He turned to her in a manner which begged a quiet banishment of the subject.

"It suggests something," he said, "but it doesn't prove anything. And now that it's stopped raining—"

"Yes. We'll go on. I know a place for tea. But—Roger."

"Yes?"

"I'm worried about you in that house."

"You needn't be. I can look after myself. I don't want you to worry about me, but I'm somehow glad you do. That sounds odd, doesn't it? Come along."

They walked on under a sky which broke into blue a labyrinth of lanes came to one which ended in a high road and cars passing either way across the top. They turned to the right. At the end of half a mile there was a road-house, and a few cars standing in the pull-in before it.

Tea came to them in an atmosphere of stock-jobbing, golf and leisured nonentities—Surbiton *in rure,* Roger called it—which was at least earthy and shadow- dispelling.

Afterwards he was her companion as far as the Vicaragp, where he declined an invitation to the house but walked with her a yard or two inside the gate.

"Goodbye, Marjory dear," he said, "and thanks very much."

"What for?"

"Coming out with me, of course. And—I'm remembering what you said."

"What was that?"

" 'I think,' he quoted 'if I were in love and sure that he was in love with me, the happiest time would be then —before we ever spoke of it. Or that would be the happiest time to look back upon.' "

"Goodbye," said Marjory. "Run along."

"Right! Well, I'm not going to say anything after that. Not say anything, you know. But—have you been happy just for a moment or two this afternoon?"

She demurred, looking down.

"I could tell you," she said, "without saying anything; and if I do will you promise to run straight away without saying another word?"

"Yes. Without another word."

Her hand was still in his. She hesitated—or seemed to hesitate—another moment or two, leaving him to wonder what she meant.

Suddenly she turned her face and put up a little flushed cheek. Roger bent quickly. A second later she slipped her hand from his and turned to hurry up the path almost at a run.

"Goodbye, Roger," she called, without looking round. "See you soon."

He stood watching her in silence, suddenly and vastly happy.

CHAPTER XVI
TERROR IN THE LIBRARY

"Trode is a trifle remiss this evening," Garrow remarked, as Trode stood at Roger's elbow, filling his glass with port from a cradled bottle. "He has not offered you the walnuts."

Trode, as if telepathetically aware that he had been mentioned, lifted his gaze. Garrow made rapid motions with his fingers and Trode, with an inarticulate croak of apology, made good the omission. He caught his master's glance once more, bowed silently, and withdrew from the room.

"Well," Garrow resumed, "unless I am deceived you had a most pleasant afternoon. Did you hear any more news about—er—that terrible affair?"

"No," said Roger; "I suppose it is much too early yet. And incidentally the weather was extremely showery." He paused and smiled to himself. "What makes you say that I had a pleasant afternoon?"

"Come," said Garrow, gently challenging in tone and smile. "Hadn't you?"

"Quite—but what makes you think it? Am I looking so pleased with myself?"

"No. You wear the every-day air of polite misery to which my society is no doubt conducive. However, I do not speak idly. Let me think a moment as to how I can best convey a delicate hint."

Garrow was silent for a moment and touched his brow with slim, white, attenuated fingers.

"It was a pity," he said presently, in his slow, gentle voice, "that young Bodding happened along just when he did."

Roger at first answered only with a slow stare. Speech came soon after Garrow's sudden laughter.

"Bodding? Oh, yes, I know the man you mean. He saw me talking to a lady in a lane. You don't mean to say that he dashed down here and told you?"

Garrow laughed again.

"My dear fellow, when you've a hundred pounds to spare, just offer it to young Bodding and see if it will induce him to call here even in broad daylight and tell me anything at all. I don't think you'd lose your money."

"You mean they are all afraid of you?" Roger knew enough not to doubt it. "But why?"

"It isn't for us to probe the brains of fools. You see that walnut. Would you have cracked it if you had known that it contained no more than a little greenish dust?"

"I think," said Roger, "that you like to be considered mysterious and have people afraid of you."

"I don't like nor dislike. As regards the world in general and its attitude towards me I have long-since achieved a Nirvana-like state of indifference."

"You haven't yet told me how you knew the—er— the quite trivial incident you have just mentioned. You couldn't have been passing that way because—"

"My dear fellow, I have not left the house. Nor have I seen anybody but Trode, who has also been within doors all the afternoon."

"Then how did you know?"

Dr. Garrow eyed him sidelong and quizzically.

"My dear fellow," he said again, "when you were very small and had done something wrong your elders had an infallible means of bringing it home to you. A Little Bird told them. I—well, I find it desirable, even necessary, to keep a number of such little birds."

"Seriously, though?" said Roger.

"Oh, seriously; I may one day communicate one or two small secrets to you. I say 'may' advisedly. It depends on your aptitude. At present you show no sign of being a likely initiate."
Roger laughed. It seemed to him that it amused Garrow for the passing while to puzzle him and he had no objection to fall in with the mood.

"Are you talking of magic?" he asked lightly.

"Dear me, what is that? Oh, yes, I know the word. Carelessly I may have used it. It is become a silly word, invariably misused or misapplied. Cheap conjurors are very fond of it. It means—if anything at all—the lore of the Magi who knew, no doubt, more than they divulged, but were certainly not conjurors. Nothing can happen without the will of one of the great Rival Forces, of which one is commonly called Good and the other Evil. In Nature the two are at enmity and yet strangely commingled."

"Obviously," said Roger, who thought that at this juncture a word was demanded, while at the same time more than one might prove too many.

"Very well. It is no use for the man who would have Knowledge—another name for Science, as you need not be reminded—to try to wrest it from the eternal battlefield of Nature. He must join one Force or the other. Let us see what the opposing Generals have to offer him.

"The one promises him nothing in this world, but gives him a vague hope of indescribable happiness in the next. His enemy, properly approached, can be made to offer him all he wants on earth."

Roger wanted to laugh. He had heard the same argument applied—with a very different motive—in a Sunday School sermon when he was ten. He snatched at a memory of that sermon in replying.

"Yes, and for how long?" he said. "About seventy years."

Dr. Garrow laughed.

"Why not seven hundred thousand years? Our solar system is probably good enough for that. Or seven million years. Nobody knows. And for that time a man can live the earth—life if he desire it—and if he seek the means."

Roger laughed this time, but very politely.

"Don't all of us poor children want to go to bed when we're tired?"

"Yes—but who wants to be tired? If, while we lived, a means could be found to lift the burden of the years, and keep it raised—"

Dr. Garrow was smiling all the time, and Roger now laughed openly without fear of hurting the feelings of a lunatic. The man was only joking after all, and leading him in fun into these labyrinths of preposterous surmise.

"Dr Faustus," Roger suggested, laughing.

"Precisely. And there is a great deal more truth in that old Rhineland legend than most people suppose. I do not mean that Faustus went in flames through a trapdoor when his term of years was ended—to the consternation and moral uplift of the pit and gallery. But I believe that he existed and I believe that he was coerced into a one-sided bargain. As regards the single factor of Time, he did not ask enough."

Roger laughed again.

"Oh, well," he said, "I suppose if he had played his hand better, he might have been alive to-day, a potentate of unlimited wealth and power. Wouldn't it be a world!"

"Would it not! And you have just struck another nail on the head. Who would be condemned to crawl through this world's history in obscurity and poverty? Oh, no! One would require unlimited wealth."

"And, of course," said Roger, who could not keep his irony too light, "one would not be asking very much!" Garrow laughed. He seemed now to be thoroughly enjoying the game he had begun.

"Very much, eh? Too much, you think? It is all relative. You go to an hotel with a few pounds in your pocket and order a good meal, and you are not asking too much of the proprietor. The tramp who crawls into the cheap eating-house with insufficient coppers to pay for his rough meal is asking too much. And that, without irony, is true enough. The tramp should learn the means of dining as delicately as you, and paying for his meal. The means are there—if he would seek them." Dr. Garrow's last words were uttered in a tone and manner different from those which preceded them. In Roger's imagination, tainted suddenly by thoughts unbidden and unformed, they seemed to linger on the air like the stench of blown-out candles. He spoke in a tone which he thought, and hoped, might cause some slight measure of offence.

"Haven't we gone back again to dear old Faust?" he asked.

"I did not know that we had left him," said Dr. Garrow. "I seemed to notice some continuity in our talk— or at least in my share of it. Are you ready? I will give you just two games of chess if you feel inclined." He rose and Roger followed him to the door, where Dr. Garrow paused to give him precedence.

They said little in the library. Dr. Garrow won both games like an incarnate Nemesis, and at the conclusion of the second rose smiling softly to himself before Roger realised that the game was really over. He sat for a few moments studying the board, while Dr. Garrow sauntered across the room.

"Yes," said Roger, "it looks like mate."

"Very much like mate," said Garrow, turning. "I am off now. Good night and sleep well. I trust you generally do. Are you coming along now?"

Roger knew his cue and felt it as well to humour the man. He could read or write in his own room if he felt disposed.

"Yes, I think so," he said, rising.

Garrow, still half turned towards him, smiled for the first time since he had administered the little snub downstairs.

"That's right,"'he said, with sudden gentleness, "get all the sleep you can. There are those who know no rest, nor will ever know it; no rest at all."

For the first time in Roger's experience a note of pathos had crept into Garrow's voice, and in Roger's ears it sounded more than a murmur wrung from the flesh for weariness of the body and mind. It was like the echo of a hopeless cry of men shipwrecked and doomed, borne across leaping waters by the gale.

Roger, in his own room, had no will to read and doubted his power to sleep. He needed the society and talk of comfortable friends to drive out uncomfortable thoughts.

Having clambered into bed he lay thinking and broad awake for upwards of half an hour, and at last leaned out and groped for his dinner jacket.

He expected to find in the breast pocket the solace of most sleepless men; and not until his hand fumbled upon a silk lining that felt flat and empty did he remember that he had left his cigarettes in the library. After a minute's irresolution he climbed out of bed and put on his dressing-gown and slippers. Then he crept out and along the corridor.

His passage through the silent house began—as later he owned to himself—with that sensation which has long since become the cause of a cliche. Roger, in describing it later, and having turned his mind inside out for a phrase unlikely to offend an educated mind, despaired and called it "dreamlike unreality." At least he was understood.

He was conscious, in the first place of rhythmic sounds, slow and softly crisp. They reminded him on the instant of the sounds made by somebody sweeping a carpet. He drew nearer to them as he drew nearer to the library door. Surprised conjecture spoke, as it were, with a shrug, murmuring, "Trode at work at this hour!"

He opened the library door—not upon darkness, but upon strong moonlight from the open windows. Something was moving rhythmically to and fro across an open space. Undoubtedly it was a broom, but the hands which held it, the head, body and limbs of the being who directed it, were alike invisible.

Roger heard himself cry out. The broom dropped with a crash as if the Invisible Hands had let it fall, and Roger turned with—it seemed to his smashed and shattered consciousness—the Powers of Hell racing at his heels and all their voices raving in his ears. Then came the merciful Dark.

He woke in bed—and Trode in the room with his tea. Roger, a sweat still upon him, turned a white and drawn face upon the deaf mute, who set down the tray, grunted unintelligibly and stooped to pick something from the floor.

Then, with another grunt, he laid it on the tray beside -the teapot.

It was Roger's cigarette case.

CHAPTER XVII
LOVE—AND CHAMPAGNE

Roger lay, his tea untasted, letting the cigarette case grow warm in his hands. He had heard often enough, and sometimes used, the homely expression, "You must have dreamed it." But never had he used or taken it literally. Dreams, with him, had hitherto been easily identified as dreams from the first moment of waking. Never before had he had the preternaturally vivid dream which left memory charged with minute details and wrought an impression so coloured as to become a counterfeit of memory.

He had met those who claimed a similar experience and never quite believed them. Now he was willing to apologise. He had -had the same experience. Ergo it was possible after all.

It is the natural way, when faced with a surprising but established fact, to try to discover the cause. He made that effort now, propped on an elbow and frowning over his cooling tea. He was a worried man, living in an atmosphere of mystery.

There was that strange creature, Garrow; the hardly less peculiar creature, Trode; the vanished corpse; the vanished sailor; the murder of Smith. A man, living in such an atmosphere, might well excuse his subconsciousness for spewing up its horror in a vile dream which bore the colours and form of fact.

Yet, if it amounted to that, he could be astonished that the horrors of the dream were comparatively mild. He had dreamed more horribly, although less realistically, on account of a heavy supper or a trivial worry.

But all speculations, with regard to dreams, tend to lead one only into 'trackless regions of utter darkness. The doctors can give glib assurance to the effect: "You dreamed this because you have experienced That and so you will dream The Other"—with more than one chance in a million of proving a true prophet.

However he looked at it—he told himself—he had obviously been dreaming. Brooms do not sweep floors of their own volition. Therefore he had dreamed. Therefore he was not well. Therefore—He dropped out of bed and looked at himself in the glass. Certainly he did not look very well; but one- hardly expects to look well on the morning after nightmare. He told the face in the glass that It had been worrying too much over matters which did not concern It; and the face in the glass agreed with him so cordially that surmise became established fact.

"Bath and breakfast," thought Roger, turning away. ' "And then, for God's sake, a little sanity."

But even in broad daylight, even while his cold skin tingled and warmed under the rough towel, the echoes of unanswered questions reiterated in a sombre region of the mind. Who *did* keep the house clean? Nightmare had suggested a broom working of its own volition. Nightmare had unlocked a dusty closet and loosened twilight memories of Grimm and Hans Anderson. Sub- consciousness, with the reins dropped had galloped straight to the impossible. But that faculty which he called Common or Garden Horse Sense had for him no answer at all.

He was in the habit of smoking while he worked, and he was an untidy smoker. Once he was absorbed the sight of an ash tray rarely made any silent suggestion. Always at night he left a little ash on the floor of the library; always in the morning the floor was clean. Trode? Well, Trode could scarcely do everything. And there was Garrow's hint about servants whom he was unlikely to see. What, in the name of Sanity, was meant by that?

The answer to that last question might lie in the fact that Garrow seemingly loved to be mysterious. He evaded questions, open or implied, with a kind of intellectual coquetry. It might be that he was a sphinx without a secret, a vain and silly old man who enjoyed living in an aura of mystery. If so, the fortuitous happenings around him—if fortuitous they were—were of vast assistance to the pose.

That morning, shortly before eleven, Roger found occasion to go out and post a letter. It had become almost a regular habit and, more often than not, he found the person to whom it was addressed, waiting outside or standing at the counter within.

This morning the Person was waiting for him—to the private entertainment of certain village ladies, who dropped their dusters and sidled behind muslin window curtains with the air of Amazon bandits lying in ambush. These fairly regular meetings between Marjory and Roger provided much food for discussion at the Women's Institute, over cups of tea in kitchens, at street corners, and beside the counters of shops. "Miss Marjory gettin' off with *him*—and before everybody's eyes! A man out of *that* house! I wonder her Dad allows it. And him a clergyman, too!"

And Miss Marjory, quite well aware of the criticism she had evoked, thought of telling remarks to have ready should anyone venture to let fall an impertinent hint.

"Good morning, Roger."

"Good morning, me child, how are you? You're looking well."

"Don't call me that," she laughed. "I hate it. It sounds like some horrible old actor doing the Heavy. Well, I can't say the same for you. You don't look a bit fit. What's the matter?"

"Nothing, thanks. I'm all right."

"Now, now!" She had begun to laugh. "Do you know what happens to little boys who don't tell the truth?"

"They go and live with Dr. Garrow, I daresay. No, I'm all right, Marjory. Had a bit of a nightmare last night, that's all."

"I don't wonder at it—in that house! What did you dream?"

"Are you interested in people's dreams?"

"Awfully. I tell all mine to old Mrs. Cook at Deepdene and she interprets them for me. It makes Father perfectly furious—because he can't get over or round the fact that people in the Bible used to have their dreams interpreted. What was yours? and when I see her—" Roger laughed and shook his head.

"No, you don't," he said. "I don't want to have anything to do with any more crazy people. I'm a borderline case myself already, if I'm not completely ga-ga."

"Well, tell me."

He laughed and told her, making light of it. Marjory smiled, and for a moment her gaze travelled past him and went into the distance.

"But who really does all the housework?"

"Trode, I suppose. Yet I can't think how. Dr. Garrow once babbled about other servants that I wasn't likely to see; but I don't see how he can keep 'em locked up all day and let 'em loose at night."

Marjory eyed him in silence for a moment.

"Why don't you sit up one night and see?" she suggested; and then on a sudden impulse altered her tone. "No, don't!" she amended hastily, dropping her little gloved hand on his sleeve.

"I'd rather you didn't," she said vaguely.

"Well, I haven't—because for one thing it's hardly my business, and for another, my queer employer wants me to go to bed—or rather to my bedroom—pretty early."

"Yes. Well, Roger?"

Her eyes, dark with meaning, held his for a moment. He wavered a little and laughed uncomfortably.

"Yes? Well?" he said.

"Doesn't that suggest something to you?"

"Suggest what?"

"That there's something queer going on. Worse than queer."

He felt suddenly as if a cold hand had touched him. "I wish you hadn't said that," he muttered.
"What do you mean?"

"I'm not going to say it. Roger, dear—I'm sorry, that slipped out—I'd only seen you once before you .came here; but I'd always thought of you as a sort of—well, a sort of relative, because of Reggie—"

"Marjory dear, go on calling me Roger dear—but not because of Reggie."

She laughed a little in spite of herself.

"Don't try to put me off. I mean—I was going to say —we're, not awfully poor. I've talked it over with the People. Won't you let Father lend you something to tide you over until you can get another job. We want you out of that house. I know, I feel—I think we all feel—that something ghastly is going to happen there." He did not answer. Instead he said gruffly: "I'll walk with you a little way, if you don't mind."

"While you think it over?" she asked hopefully.

"Not exactly. In fact, I've thought it over."

She had turned in the direction of the Vicarage and they fell into step. They were walking between hedges before either spoke.

"Well?" she said. "You said you'd thought it over."

"Yes; and of course I'm staying on. At least for the present."

"Roger!"

"Wait a moment. What do you think of me?"

"I don't know what you mean."

"Yes, you do. What *would* you think of me, I mean? I don't think I'm quite a funk, but I haven't been tested yet. Not really tested. You wouldn't think a lot of me if I ran away."

She hesitated only for a moment.

"I should—if I asked you." There was a pause, and then she spoke in another tone. "Besides, what would it matter to you what I thought?"

They were passing a gateway set deep in the hedge beside them. He drew her to the gate where they stood hidden from the long stretches of road before and behind.

"Everything," he said. "I've no right to say it—I'm not in a position to say it—and I shan't say it at all well. I'm no good at this sort of thing. But—I happen to love you."

Having said it he frowned and looked down upon dry Mother Earth, scarred and dented with the hoofs of cattle, so that he did not see a sudden and deeper warmth of colouring nor the soft glow in hazel eyes. A small voice spoke close to his heart.

"Do you, dear? I'm so glad."

Roger was no longer uncertain of what to do. Next moment she was in his arms, and she remained thus for two minutes until the humming of a car along the road brought the unwelcome release.

"You know," said Roger, sheepishly, "there's a lot to be said for cars that make a noise. Now if that had been a Rolls—"

"Darling," said Marjory, almost piteously, "you're not going to talk about cars now?"

She was in his arms again, laughing up at him, the flush now beginning to die. He laughed happily, but quite helplessly.

"Dearest," he muttered, "you've got to excuse me. I don't know what to say. I've told you I love you."

"Then tell me again—you idiot!"

"I love you."

"That's better."

"Do you—just the least bit—?"

"Do you think I should want to hear you say that if I didn't?"

Roger woke to a strong probability which, to his dazed intelligence, was still something short of established fact. "Well, we're engaged to be married," he said simply. Marjory had completely regained her composure. "That's what I thought," she said laughing, "presuming your intentions to be honourable."

Ten minutes later, still standing by the gate, some degree of clarity returned to Roger's mind.

"Let's talk this over," he said. "Do you mind if I don't look at you for the time being?"

"Why shouldn't you?"

"Because when I look at you I want to kiss you, and I can't think of anything else."
"Then keep on—no, don't. What did you want me to say?"

"Well, first of all, you know I haven't a bean. How are your people going to take this?"

"I've had a hint or two. They think it's happened already, only we've kept quiet."

"Well, they ought to know you better than that—even if they don't know me. Well, look here, I've got a pound or two. A few pounds and I can leave this Job—which is wearing me down a bit—and look for something else."

"Ah!" cried Marjory, and clapped her hands.

"But I'm not going to be in a hurry. I'm going to find the other job first. Then we can get married right away."

"Who said so?" she laughed.

"Presuming your intentions to be honourable," he quoted.

"I've a little money," said Marjory. "Not enough to keep us both, but—"

"S'sh."

"But about enough to clothe myself and pay the rent of a modest house, or a flat in town. If you can provide the food and keep the Plain Vans at bay. I'll tell you what—don't come up to the house now. Come up this afternoon. I'll talk it over with the People first."

Roger hesitated.

"Are you sure you'd rather do that?"

"Yes—I think so. Not that it will be a surprise to them. They're both making jokes at me. They're awfully fond of you, you know. Then by the time you see them—"

"Father will have his big boots on!"

Marjory uttered a little gay laugh.

"Don't be silly. We shall all have had time to discuss ways and means. And this afternoon we won't be at home to anybody but you. And now, my dear, you'd better be going back, or that Monster in Human Form—"

"I'm not going to leave you this morning for all the Monsters in Human Form."

"Yes, you are, my dear. Keep the Beast in a good temper."

"Who cares?"

"Well, don't, then." Inspiration had dawned in her eyes. "Come and stay to lunch now and spend the day—." She was a little too transparent and he saw and laughed.

"Yes—and get shopped. That's what you're angling for, young woman. Well, you can't have it both ways. I think I'll keep the Beast in a good temper and come up this afternoon. Now where can we say Goodbye?"

"There's another gate in the hedge just around the bend," she said; "and nearly every evening there's a couple saying Goodbye there. Two or three hours it very often takes them, and it used to surprise me. That was before I knew how nice it was."

Marjory smiled.

"Nice? To say Goodbye?"

"Yes, dear—when it's for such a very little while."

It was almost lunch time when Roger returned. He went down when he had heard the gong rumble, and it seemed that, as usual, he was to lunch alone. There was no soup. Trode served him with smoked salmon and went behind him to the sideboard. A moment later Roger heard the unmistakeable explosion of a champagne cork.

Trode brought the brimming glass and the depleted bottle of Pol Roger to Roger's right elbow, and while Roger's eyebrows went up at the sight of champagne— masked and unexpected—Trode wrote hastily on a postcard and laid it where Roger could read:

"Dr. Garrow's comp'ments, and he hopes as this is the approprit wine for drinking a certain party's health on this happy occashin."

Roger sat staring at the card while the untasted wine foamed in the glass beside him. It was as if he had stepped suddenly into darkness out of light. To himself, to the deaf man beside him, to the empty air, he blurted out aloud the unanswered question:

"How the devil does Dr. Garrow know?"

CHAPTER XVIII
ANOTHER STRAW?

It was the Rev. Vallence himself who admitted Roger when he arrived that afternoon—or rather invited him to enter, for the door stood open in the sunlight and the Vicar was in the act of crossing the hall as Roger mounted the steps.

"Come in, come in. What a lovely afternoon. You want to see Marjory, I suppose? Well, you can't."

Roger crossed the threshold.

"Is she out?" he asked, slightly surprised.

"No—in. Very much in." Vallence was portentously serious. "I locked her in one of the attics—after something she told me. Bread and water. The old-fashioned method, you know."

Roger caught the sudden twinkle before Vallence grinned openly and delightedly. They both laughed.

"They're in the garden, I think," Vallence continued. "Come in here and take a pew. We're all awfully pleased —so you needn't look like a dog that's going to have a bath. But I know what it's like. I've been through the same sort of thing myself three or four times. *Your* end of it, I mean."

"Three of four times!" said Roger, grinning.

"You need not mention that to the Mistress of the House," said the Vicar with mock austerity. "She wasn't the first. Thank God she's been the last. Well, my dear fellow, this isn't exactly a surprise—or, rather, if there is an element of surprise it's a pleasant one. We knew Marjory was fond of you. I'm glad you responded." He was piloting Roger by the arm.

"Wretched for a girl—when she gives her heart where it isn't wanted. She can't do anything, can't say anything. And if she lets people guess she feels a fool. A man can at least get it off his chest to the one person concerned without any loss of dignity. Well, my dear fellow, I hope you'll both be very happy."

"Thanks awfully," said Roger, like a boy. He hastened to cover that which he felt to be an infelicitous reply. "You're not the first to congratulate me, you know."

Vallence stared at the younger man in frank surprise. "Good Lord! Whom have you been telling?"

"Nobody; but I had this message from Garrow at lunch time." He was taking the card from his pocket. "Look."

"That devil!" said Vallence through a mouth that suddenly hardened. "When did you see him?"

"I haven't seen him at all to-day. I tell you—after I left Marjory this morning I went back to lunch, and Trode wrote this message from his master, and incidentally brought me a bottle of champagne. So what do you make of it?"

"This—my dear fellow—that you are going, to get out of that house. Don't go back."

"I must. I'm all right. What harm can I come to? What harm dare he do? If anything happened to me you'd pretty soon set inquiries in motion—and he knows it. But I'm beginning to believe—to think—" He broke off. "Did Marjory tell you about my dream? The broom, you know."

"Yes. *Was* it a dream?"

"It must have been. But I've got to find some way to convince myself. I've been afraid of going off my head. It isn't, pleasant to have to try hard to persuade oneself that one hasn't seen the impossible."

Vallence lit a cigarette.

"What do you call the impossible, young man? Go back into history a little—obscure history, I grant you— and read for yourself of the people in the Middle Ages, mostly women, who were condemned for witchcraft on their own confessions."

"Wrung from them by torture, surely?" said Roger. "Not always. Not always by any means. And, besides, confession meant burning. There are still relics of it in the country, particularly in Cornwall and Wales. The folk there are clumsy dabblers, but they get results—of a kind. There was a woman here once."

He paused and grimaced.

"They sent for me when she was dying, but she was gone before I arrived. They'd opened the front of her nightdress and I saw the Marks."

"What Marks?" Roger inquired.

The Vicar looked pointedly at him for a moment without speaking.

"And now, Roger," he said, "let's try to look into the future a little way. What do you mean to do? You won't get another queer job like this. Try school- mastering again?"

Roger heard only about half of this. He was still pondering the ominous closure of the previous topic.

"I beg your pardon? I don't know. I haven't really thought. It's a dead end."

"All ends are dead. An old friend of mine, Canon Vanston, has just been appointed headmaster of Mine- stead. He'd take you on my recommendation, I'm sure, as soon as there's a vacancy. I don't suppose you'd get more than two-fifty or three hundred at first. But I'm sure Vanston would see that you got a House in time. Then, my dear fellow, you begin to make money."

"As a scholastic doss-house proprietor," Roger laughed, "and Marjory the landlady. I can't see Marjory in that narrow circle, drinking tea with the other masters' wives, and conspiring to down some poor devil of an ush because he's plain and shy and unsociable and 'not quite a sahib'. Would she stick it?"

Vallence smiled.

"I think she'd put up with a great deal more than that. Ask her. And if you can stand living with Dr. Garrow—"

Roger's spontaneous laugh broke in.

"You're right, Mr. Vallence. I'll take the job if you can get it for me. And meanwhile—"

"Meanwhile, why not come and make your home with us?"

"That's much too good of you, but I mustn't think of it. I've got a little money now. I've had to spend next to nothing. If I stay on another six weeks I can last out for quite a time. Besides—"

"Well?" said Vallence."

Roger hesitated.

"I don't exactly know how to put it. I'm in a queer business, and I don't want to come out of it leaving it queer. Ethically speaking, how do I stand? Let's suppose the incredible—that Dr. Garrow is in league with the Powers of Darkness. Am I right in taking his money with one hand and trying to down him with the other?" Vallence's eyes narrowed.

"My dear boy, if you find a burglar in your bedroom you don't go downstairs to find boxing gloves before you hit him. But that's beside the point. For all our sakes I want you out of that house."
"And I want to get out." He paused and lit another cigarette. "But just to be paradoxical I want to stay— a little longer."

"Why?"

"I've begun something and I want to see the end." Sheer, vulgar curiosity."

Vallence laughed without mirth in acknowledgment of a frank admission. Then he rose.

"Come along, my weak brother," he said. "Let's find Marjory and her mother."

They were in the garden at the back of the Vicarage. Marjory came hurrying forward, her face radiant.

"Not even a black eye," she said. "Father's been scamping his job." She turned to her father. "Isn't this where you say 'Bless you, my children?' "

"Or something like it. Life at the best is very hard, and the best of us go through it punching and clawing at one another. Don't hurt each other more than you can help."

Mrs. Vallence came and took Roger's hand and put up her face to be kissed. She was laughing and unusually vivacious, but there was the least hint of moisture in her eyes.

"Dear Roger, I'm so pleased. Be very good to her, won't you?"

Roger, the prospective thief of a daughter, understood. He swallowed before answering. "I'll try."

It was neither a long speech nor eloquent. But it was exactly all that was required of him.

Five minutes later they heard a movement of the glass door of the house, and all three turned to see the maid set foot on the gravel, cross the path and come hurrying towards them. Vallence frowned as the girl approached.

"Somebody for me, Nelly? I told you definitely that I am not at—that is to say—I am engaged for the afternoon."

"I'm sorry, sir," The girl looked troubled. "I think you'd better come. It's a tramp."

"What? Won't he go away?"

"It isn't that, sir. He's ill. I'm sure he isn't shamming. He went all white and caught hold of the side of the door. I didn't know what to do, so I let him sit in the hall."

Roger bit his lip. He had a private—and it proved unfounded—suspicion that by this time there was no tramp in the hall and something missing from the umbrella stand.

"I'll go to him," said Vallence simply.

They all returned to the house through the glass door. Vallence went out into the hall and presently called Roger. Roger went out and saw him standing with an air of concern beside a shabby man sprawling in a chair. The stranger's face was a yellowish mask, the eyes slightly dilated and the mouth opened and closed jerkily in the labour of breathing.

"Roger," said the Vicar over his shoulder, "you'll find a little brandy in the sideboard cupboard. D'you mind?" Roger hurried. He came back with the spirit and a glass. Vallence poured some out and held the glass to the man's lips. A minute or two passed before Vallence spoke again.

"What's the matter? Hungry?"

"No, sir." The voice was deep, but a little unsteady. "I got a bad 'eart. Meanin' there's something the matter with it—if you foller me. One of these times I'll take the count altogether. Go down and stay down. And then some parish or other'll have to bury me." Vallence spoke quietly and cheerfully.

"Oh, there's plenty of life in you yet. Let me see, haven't I seen you before?"

"Yes, sir. I called' round a week or two ago. Can't seem to find no work nowhere."

"If I were you," he said, "I should give the big house a miss in baulk."

Roger spoke. Having spoken, he wondered what instinct or impulse had put the words into his mouth.

The man looked up at him sharply.

"You mean Dr. Garrow's?"

"That's right," said Roger, slightly surprised.

"You needn't tell me, sir. I went round there last time after I'd been here. Queer place it is—and queer people."

"In what way?" Vallence prompted him.

"That's more'n I know. The old toff seemed very kind. He give me a shilling and then asked me where I was making for. I wasn't makin' for anywhere in particular, so I told him a town some long ways off. So he starts in to tell me that I'd never get there that night. Then he said as he was goin' out and wouldn't be back until late; but if I liked to come back about eleven he'd see me and let me sleep in the empty coach-house, and I could have some breakfast in the morning."

"Well?"

"Well, it seemed all right. Better'n Mrs. Greenfield's. And then he started in to tell me that I mustn't let on to nobody, because, he said, he'd be gettin' lots of fellers like me. So I goes orf, and presently I lies down under a tree in a field and has a doss. And I dreamed of my old mother.

"I don't know as I'd dreamed of her more'n two-three times since she died; but I see her as plain as I see you two gentlemen. Ah, and I heard her talk, too, same like in life.

"Askin' your pardon, your reverence, for repeatin' just what she said—but she was one of the 'omely sort, bless her, and swearin' come to 'er quite natural like. 'Don't you go near that b----- man,' she says, 'or he'll cut out your b---- liver with a b---- great carving knife.' That what she says, and I can 'ear her sayin' it now.

"Well, after a bit I woke up and I felt proper lousy. That dream 'ad got me groggy. I'd never known the old lady let me down. I couldn't get it out of my 'ead that that dream 'ad come as a sort o' warnin'—like that gentleman in the Bible who dreamed of the ten thin cows. And—well, I didn't go back, and some'ow I don't fancy calling there again."

The Vicar threw Roger a swift glance.

"I don't know that I blame you," he said. "Roger, my dear fellow, do you mind lending me sixpence? I've nothing on me but two half crowns, and really I can't afford—"

Roger produced two sixpences.

"One from each of us," he said. "No, I don't think I should call on Dr. Garrow. He might remember you and ask you why you didn't come back on that other occasion."

Five minutes later the man, recovered enough to continue his lifelong, questless pilgrimage, went lurching slowly down the drive. Roger looked after him, aware of a certain tension in the atmosphere.

A hand fell on his shoulder. Vallence spoke quietly into his ear.

"Well, Roger, my boy? Was that another straw in the wind?"

CHAPTER XIX
THE VOICE

Dr. Garrow came downstairs into the hall in his purple robe a minute or two before Trode came out to beat the gong for the second time that evening. Roger was sitting waiting and rose at the sound of footfalls. Garrow patted the air with his hand and smiled, but Roger waited for him, standing.

"Well," said Garrow, with a wide smile, "you received my felicitations by proxy. And I trust you drank the lady's health. I must confess that I was too deeply engrossed at the time to join you and offer verbal congratulations—as I do now. For myself, I am not much of a marrying man. Of course, I have sampled matrimony. An open-minded man should be ever willing to try any reasonable experiment. It suits ninety-eight per cent of the human race, although seventy-five per cent of the experimentalists would not agree with me. Still they do not know.' They are unhappy married. They are unaware of the unhappiness which might have been their's had they remained single. And so—may you be happy!"

It was to the irritated Roger as if he had made this long speech for a purpose. Roger, aching in every nerve to dash in with a question, had to remain silent until it was over.

"Thank you," he said briefly. "Dr. Garrow I want to ask you a plain question. How did you know?"

Garrow was blandly innocent.

"How did I know?"

"Yes. I spoke to—" he would not mention her name to Garrow—"to a certain lady on the subject of marriage this morning. I left her and returned here for lunch. Instantly there was the kind thought of the champagne and your congratulations. Nobody had been told. I doubt if even her people had been informed by then. How did you know?"

"How did I know? How do I know that there was a slight railway accident just outside Twickenham station ten minutes ago? Nothing at all serious. Mark the time. The Wireless people will probably mention it in an hour or two, but I doubt if the news has reached them yet. Just a little damage done to rolling stock and two people bumped their heads. It will probably be in the paper tomorrow—in a very small paragraph. It is ten to eight now. The accident occurred roughly at seven-forty. Would you care to bet me a shilling?"

"Very well," said Roger laughing. "The odds in my favour run into millions."

"On the contrary. The odds are in my favour, but only to the extent of about fifty to one. There is just the chance that the accident having been so slight, the inch or two of space originally allotted to it may be given to some more important happening. A professional cricketer may have fallen off his bicycle, or a three- legged fowl may have been hatched in Rudgwick. One can never tell."

Roger laughed, and shook his head.

"That—excuse me—allows rather a wide loop-hole."

"Why, so it does. Were I in your place I think I should write to the Southern Railway and inquire. However, I thought I had told you enough concerning your own doings to convince you that I do not rely on guesswork."

The tone was one of light banter. Roger replied in kind, half believing his own words. He laughed in speaking.

"Look here, Dr. Garrow. You love to mystify, and I own that you do it very well. I think I know your methods. You knew—or guessed—that I was attached to somebody. Unseen by me, you happened to notice my coming back to the house at lunch time. You saw that I was looking happy, as in fact I was. You put two and two together and came to the inevitable four. Hence your kindly note. Am I not right?"

Dr. Garrow wafted the subject away with a careless Hand.

"Oh, as you like, as you like. The professional conjuror is a dull dog as soon as he has explained his tricks. Watson, having listened to the deductions of Holmes, was more amazed at his own blindness than at his friend's deductive faculty. That at least is truth labouring in fiction. Let us say that I am a foolish old man— although something of a scholar, if you will grant so much—who loves to mystify. Ah, here comes the excellent Trode. From which we deduce that dinner is ready."

The white-faced servant came hurrying into the hall, at first apparently unaware of his master's presence, and approached the gong. Garow fixed his gaze on Trode's back, and the man suddenly faltered, hesitated and turned. Garrow pointed to the gong and shook his head. The man bowed and hurried out again through the baize- covered door which gave access to the kitchen and servants' quarters.

"Come along," said Garrow, smiling. "After dinner you may give me just one game of chess. And then you may run away and dream of somebody. *Et ego in Arcaria vixt.*"

"I thought you said you hadn't," Roger remarked as he rose.

Dr. Garrow lingered, making a tentative and quickly abandoned gesture as if to link arms with him.

"Because you thought me cynical about the highly essential attraction between men and women which is called Love? But no. I have condemned nothing untried. When one is thirsty a rough wine tastes like a vintage. Don't begin to think now of ten years hence, but come and tell me ten years hence. There is one wine which does not pay for keeping—even for a very short count of years."

A great weariness had crept into his voice again. For no fathomable reason it brought back into Roger's mind a memory of that sad, proud face seen in the crystal— his own reflection, blurred and distorted, or was it some other face? Roger, walking a little in advance, heard the Doctor humming and murmuring:

'"Then come kiss me, Sweet and Twenty—
Youth's a stuff will not endure."

Garrow paused and piloted Roger before him into the room with a light touch on the shoulder.

"And he knew something, that poor devil Shakespeare, married to the worst shrew in Warwickshire—scraggy mutton so much older than himself—in order to give her child a name."

"Was she a shrew?" Roger asked, half turning. "I didn't know."

"Was she a shrew! My dear fellow, you should have heard her that afternoon when the Players were setting up their stage in the yard of the Nag's Head at Barking.

"I don't know the incident," said Roger, smiling, "and it almost sounds as if you were present."

"And if you knew as much as I do you wouldn't be so sure that *you* were not there. I remember weeping when I heard that he who wrote of Dr. Faustus—he who would have been a better man than Will—dropped in the gutter of Cheapside with a bradawl in his guts."

"You're a reincarnation, I suppose," said Roger in a voice which tact had rendered almost toneless. Simultaneously came the thought, "mad as Bedlam," accompanied by the mental shrug.

"When you know me a little better I shall not have to tell you."

Roger was silent. Garrow went to his place at the head of the table.

"When you know me a little better," he repeated, "I shall not have to tell you—when I am taking a rise out of you."

He wheezed with sudden laughter, almost silent and wholly delighted. Roger's answering smile was faint, and polite rather than spontaneous. He could have kicked himself. It was Dr. Garrow's way. He talked like a madman and then suddenly turned upon his hearer and laughed because he had been taken to mean his own nonsense.

It seemed to Roger that in a game of this sort between them the odds were not fair. Garrow employed him and Garrow was by a great deal his senior. He could not say to Garrow: "Shut up, you damned old fool, and don't talk like a lunatic." And Garrow, himself alive to the situation, was taking an unfair advantage of his position.

Garrow, seeing in his secretary a disposition to sulk—and well knowing the cause—proceeded to make amends.

"You must not mind me. I have not had much opportunity for joking for the past long while. Well, it has often amused me to imagine that I lived in the remote past. I know something of history—history, I mean, of the intimate and domestic sort. I could, in fact, pass as an authority on the seventeenth and eighteenth centuries. But enough of me. You should be a happy man this evening. Permit me to drink to the lady."

The pink face smiled across at Roger who smiled slightly in acknowledgment. Three-quarters of an hour later they had begun their game of chess, Garrow won it as usual very much as he desired. Then he turned from the board.

"I will not trespass on you any longer," he said. "You have a deal tonight to occupy your mind. Happy thoughts, I am sure. And so I leave you to them. You are going straight to your room?"

"Yes," said Roger.

"To write—Ah, but of course there is no need. It will not surprise me tomorrow to know that when you take your morning stroll you will encounter a very important person somewhere in the neighbourhood of the post office."

Roger grinned.

"You know everything," he said, without much irony. "Not quite everything, ' said Dr. Garrow modestly, "but really quite a great deal. By the way, don't forget to look in your newspaper tomorrow. The little railway accident at Twickenham, you know. I hope there will be some mention of it. And so Goodnight."

They parted outside the library door. Roger went to his room, sat down and lit a cigarette. When he had smoked it and one to follow, it would be time for him to return quietly to the library. Only by sitting there, quietly in the dark and watching for an hour or two could he rid himself of the fantastic horror of last night's dream.

More likely than not, he thought, he would see Trode—who, it would seem, slumbered so little and walked during such sleep as he permitted himself—enter with broom and dustpan and give a start of surprise to find the room still occupied.

That, however, entailed a consideration which gave Roger to pause and rub his chin. Trode no doubt would inform his master and Garrow might take >it ill. That, however, could not be helped. At the worst he could walk out with a month's money beside the amount he had already put by. It would be ample to keep him until the new scholastic year began in September; and then with the backing of his father-in-law-to-be he need not be too anxious with regard to the future.

"Damn Garrow!" he thought unaware of a passing disloyalty until conscience afterwards reproached him. "What can I tell him? I can't possibly say that I thought I'd seen a broom sweeping the floor by itself and that I'd gone back to the library tonight to make quite sure that it was a dream. He would have something pretty scathing to say to me—and I should deserve it!"

He paused in thought and grinned.

"I'll have to tell him that I went back to the library because I thought I would. Just disobeyed an order. Then, I suppose, the orchestra will begin. Well, that can't be helped. I'm going." He went. When he had reached the library and turned on the light he closed the door behind him and stood irresolute. It is difficult, as he now realised, to spy with dignity, to see without being seen, without at the same time hiding like a thief. But all he needed was one good look at the Sweeper.

On the same side of the room as the door by which he had entered was a small alcove, made deeper by the bookcase which projected in front of it. Already there was a chair there. The person who did the housework—Trode, he must suppose—would have advanced into the room too far for sudden exit by the time he became aware that the room was already occupied.

Roger sat down and tried to rally himself. He had cured himself of more than one folly by poking fun at himself. "Now," he thought, as he lit another cigarette —"now for that broom which sweeps the floor by itself. Every housewife should have one. A boon and blessing to every home." And he went on to reflect that it was generally the broom and not the sweeper which was missing; for he had read recently of a man being sent to gaol for selling phantom vacuum cleaners.

He made himself smile, but there was a shadow on his mind which lingered until he fell to thinking of Marjory, and the shadow faded.

Almost an hour and a half went by. The room remained un-tidied and un-swept. Roger had a certain eerie misgiving—at once sternly to be quelled—that his presence was already mysteriously known and that the room would be left just as it was. He was sleepy now and growing a little infirm of purpose. Something which he supposed must be Common Sense had begun to ask him of what use to sit there in the dark for nothing to happen, when he might at the same time be comfortable and asleep in bed.

He had almost surrendered to these promptings to return to his room when there happened that which caused a sudden and cold intake of breath and brought him forward in his chair with a little jerk. Without warning the latch of the door had snapped, and no doubt the handle had turned.

Roger leaned further forward so that he could peer around the edge of the alcove. He was conscious at once of movement in the semi-darkness. He was on the aperture side of the door and he saw it opening slowly inch by inch. Then in the widening aperture something moved and his strained ears caught the sound of heavy breathing.

Dusky in the vague light filtered from the night skies a man came slowly into the room. Roger knew him at once. It was Trode. Roger drew back his head. He heard the man sigh and stumble slightly and drop one hand with a rattle of unfeeling knuckles on the table. So it was true that the man walked in his sleep. Next came the problem what to do. Watch him and try to see that he came to no harm? Try to slip out without waking him and call Garrow? But the problem solved itself then and there in a manner which gave him another start and tingle of surprise. Trode had advanced some paces from the electric light switch, but Roger heard it snap and the room was suddenly illumined.

"Gratimus!"

It was Garrow's voice and it was as if the deaf man heard. He halted in his slow, fumbling gait. Roger heard the dull sounds of Garrow's footfalls upon the floor. There was a sound as if Garrow had snapped his fingers. Then silence.

Roger took another quick look. He saw the broad of Garrow's back almost obscuring Trode. The Doctor's hands were raised and moving in swift passes. He spoke again.

"Gratimus, go you into the country of the Red King. Convey to him my homage and my humble obedience. Beg of him humbly that I may have audience."

At any other time, in any other circumstance, a speech like this would have moved Roger to sudden laughter. The chill of the wave of horror which surged over him was intensified by the knowledge that for him just then there was nothing funny in it. Next moment came another shock, sharp as a blow between the eyes. Trode, the dumb man, had begun to speak. And what a voice it was!

"I see the Red King enthroned in all his pride and anguish. He speaks, but I cannot hear him."

"You cannot hear him!" Garrow repeated. "Is anything amiss?"

"I think that must be so."

Trode's voice was low and clear and had a quality which Roger could not define until afterwards. It seemed to come from a vast distance. It was as if a star had become vocal on a frosty night.

"He cannot come to you now. He shakes his head."

"Is he angry?"

"Yes, he is angry, but not, I think, with you."

"Does he desire more blood? Oh, Gratimus, tell him he shall have more blood. I must have more blood, warm blood for the dead veins before the dead mouth will speak. Tell him that, Gratimns, and beg that he protect us in the shedding of it."

There was silence a little while before Trode spoke again.

"I have told him. But only he shakes his head and frowns."

"Then what is amiss?" Garrow suddenly raised his voice in a great shout which shook Roger to his soul. "By all the Undying Fires, *is there Something with us in the room?"*

There was a sudden shriek from Trode, followed by noises bestial and indescribable. Instantly Garrow was upon him and there was a sudden swift scuffle which sent shadows swelling and leaping about the room. Roger, already half out of his chair and prepared for immediate action, suddenly understood. Trode had come out of his trance and was inarticulate once more.

Garrow was silent while the obscene and frothy mewling continued. Then Roger heard his step and lurching footfalls that stumbled and dragged; and relief came to Roger like a rush of clean air to one in the act of stifling. Garrow was leading his ceature away. There was a sudden snap and the room once more was in darkness.

Roger stood up, but instantly sat again. He was weak at the knees and suddenly he realised that his face was drenched. "Good Lord, am I bleeding?"—that thought came next. But sharp upon it came realisation. It was the sweat running down from his hair. For the moment his courage had ebbed like water from a lock and he felt weak enough for tears. He sat on, fumbling with the buttons on his waistcoat. Then after a while he rose, lurched, but found himself on serviceable if weakened limbs. He found his way to the door and stumbled out as if—and indeed feeling as if—he were dragging himself out of Hell.

"Coward! Coward!" It was his own inner voice in silent accusation. "I thought I could trust you—and you're letting me down."

He groped his way to his room, turned on the light and collapsed into a chair. This at least was no dream. He was facing stark fact—the incredible turned into devastating truth. Garrow indeed was on the Other Side. Garrow had sought the Powers of Darkness—*and not in vain.* Roger had just heard the dumb to speak, or the voice of some foul servant of the Enemy speaking with that distorted tongue.

"What now?" he asked himself. "Clear out of this tomorrow? Not I! Not my father's son! Not the man that Marjory loves! By God, no! I know which side I'm on. I'll stay and fight. I'll take his money and I'll down him. There are no laws in dealing with the like of that."
Roger rose, caught and unexpected flashing glimpse of himself in the mirror and saw his face all white and set with resolve.

"What did he mean? 'I *must have more warm blood for the dead veins before the dead mouth will speak.'* There's been bloody murder in this house."

CHAPTER XX
SUSPENCE

Roger hardly knew how to face Trode when in the morning the man brought in his tea. The memories of last night were all too recent. Even in honest daylight, with a clean wind in the room from the open window, the man's presence was repulsive. It was as if a great bat had flown in upon him from the door of a charnel house.

But Trode had something with him besides the tea. He flourished the morning paper. Evidently he had already seen Garrow and Garrow had told him to bring it.

Trode grunted and thumbed a paragraph. Roger took the paper from him and read:

"Railway mishap at Twickenham." For a moment the print swam and Roger felt slightly sick. But he began to read as Trode prepared to depart.

It was exactly as Garrow had told him. A little damage, but no serious injuries. It had happened at seven-forty and Garrow had known ten minutes afterwards.

Yes—and how? Garrow was not on the telephone, so far as Roger knew. And if he were, who would be likely to rush to a telephone and inform him of a very small mishap with which he was not in the least concerned.

Nor by any pre-arrangement—suppose Garrow had made an elaborate plan to mystify him—could the message have been delivered, since none could have foreseen the accident. The result of a race, or a match, or any such timed event, uttered by Dr. Garrow so soon afterwards would have been remarkable enough, but not entirely inexplicable.

Roger clambered out of bed while a rush of thoughts went like a torrent through his mind. "He's got that body in the house—Thurley's body—for some damned villainy. What was that which the voice coming out of Trode said last night? He murdered that poor devil of a sailor who vanished. God knows why, but I believe he did. He didn't kill poor Smith. Trode did that. Trode wasn't in the house at all at the time, although Garrow pretended to go along and talk to him. I'm beginning to see a great deal now. Quite a lot of it's getting clear. Why was Smith murdered? That's clear now—or getting clearer. Smith stole, or helped to steal, the body for him. The man had been drunk for some time on the proceeds of what Garrow gave him and there was danger that he would talk. *In vino*—well not always *verilas,* but certainly *verba.* And now—what next?"

Roger took his towel and went along to the bathroom. Immersion in cold water helped further to clear his head.

"Am I in danger?" he wondered, as he dried himself. "I don't think so. At least, not yet. If Garrow wanted me for any of his monkey tricks he's got the wrong man. If I disappeared the Vallences would soon be making a stir—some stir, too—and he knows it. He didn't know when he engaged me, but he knows it now. Then why does he still keep me? He could turn me out of the place at any moment with a month's wages."

It was as if Roger had stimulated his brain by vigorous rubbings of his scalp, for the answer came to him almost at once.

"He thinks I'd stand by him. He's afraid of a tight corner—violence. But whence? And in that event he's got—or thinks he's got—his Infernal Master on his side. The Devil looks after his own. Or doesn't he? But one would think that a man who can get brooms' to- sweep floors by themselves needn't require much protection. Besides, I'm never near him when he's up to—whatever he does get up to. I don't know. I'm damned if I know what to make of it."

Roger returned to his room to dress, still considering his position. He felt almost as powerless as a man chained and gagged watching the committal of a crime. Were he to take his story to the police they would no doubt listen to him attentively. Oh, very attentively and kindly. And then they would introduce him—and make him repeat his tale—to a most agreeable Medical Officer and his colleague, who would sign a certificate. This would entail his living in the County Asylum for the rest of his life, or for so long as the Medical Faculty thought fit.

There is a sad fellowship of men with true tales which nobody will believe and Roger found himself perilously near to joining this depressed and disgruntled Elect.

But in the midst of it all there was comfort, apart from the solace which the love of Marjory gave him. Her father—a gentleman, respected and no fool, one not altogether lacking in influence—would stand by him in any crisis. He gave Vallence the credit to think" that he would step forward and say: "I believe, and believe implicitly, Mr. Moorlock's story. There has been more than one straw in the wind to show me that this man Garrow is in league with Darkness. If Roger Moorlock is mad, then I too am mad."

Marjory was not there to meet Roger at the end of his walk that morning. He thus prolonged it and walked on to the Vicarage. His way took him past the church and, as he glanced up the path, he caught a glimpse of the Vicar's broad black back vanishing through the porch.

Roger seized an opportunity. There was a motive behind his action which he was quick to explain. He opened the gate, ran up the path and entered the church behind 5he Vicar who heard him and turned.

The Rev. Vallence smiled and nodded.

"Hullo," he said in a low voice. "Good morning."

"Good morning," answered Roger. "Excuse me—"

"Ah, you're-looking for Marjory. You will be ill- advised to find her this morning—unless you want a cold, or hay-fever or whatever it is she's got."

"Oh, isn't she well?"

"Not too well. Indisposed is, I believe, the correct word. Hay-feverish. The combined efforts of her mother and niyself persuaded her to stay at home. Once we were able to convince her that you would come up this afternoon if you didn't see her now, we extracted obedience from her. But you can go over now if you like."

He paused.

"Do you notice a smell of gas? I thought I did yesterday evening and I couldn't locate it then. I don't like gas-leaks. They're expensive even when they're not dangerous."

Roger sniffed and shook his head.

"No," he said. "I've got a pretty good nose, but I don't notice anything."

"Oh, well, I mentioned it to Brown last night and perhaps he put the matter right. A burner just turned up a little way perhaps. So now we can go. I can't smell anything either."

Roger drew nearer to him.

"Do you mind waiting just a moment, please. There's something I want to tell you."

"Here?" said Vallence in surprise.

"Yes. I'm mad, if you like. But there's somebody who has a pretty accurate idea of what goes on beyond his own normal range of sight and hearing. And—well, it did just occur to me that he mightn't be able to see in here."

"Garrow?" said Vallence, lowering his voice.

"Yes. You've made a convert in me—about that man. He told me about a very unimportant railway accident ten minutes after it had happened. But that's not the worst. That's nothing. I want to tell you about last night. He made Trode talk."

"Made Trode talk!"

"Yes. Hypnotised him, I think. I'll try to remember exactly."

Vallence indicated a pew.

"Come and sit down here. Now tell me exactly what happened. I see your idea about telling me in a church. You think he won't know—"

"I think he can't see in. Or whatever tells him—"

"It's taken you rather a long time to come round entirely to my way of thinking," said Vallence with the least hint of admonition in his voice. "Well, what happened last night?"

Roger told him. Vallence scarcely interrupted. He sat looking gravely straight before him, nodding from time to time.

"The Red Prince," he said at last—"you know who that must have been?"

"I think so."

"His god—our devil. Yes?"

"I think Trode—or something which possessed Trode —was going to warn him ot my presence. And then the fat would have-been in the fire. I don't know what would have happened. But Trode suddenly stopped being articulate and went all ga-ga. That ended the performance. Sorry, but I've got to be flippant about it, or I shall go off my head. Unless you think I'm off my head already."

"I don't. You've merely confirmed what I told you. Well? I said—well?"

Roger understood.

"Oh," he said, "I'm going to see it through—as far as I can. I'm quite powerless to thwart him, as yet. But he knows he daren't do much to me—such as arrange a fatal accident if he found me working against him—without putting his own neck into a pretty tight noose."

"Yes, but my dear fellow I am convinced that you are in peril in that house and I cannot think what may be at the back of your mind."

"I'm going to see him out of the way. Underground or safe between walls. The Law can't touch him for devil-worship—so long as he conducts it in strict privacy. But you believe—and I now believe that he's done things and may continue to do things in which the Law, if it knew, could take an extremely pertinent and active interest."

"I know. I know what you think. But I will not save it."

"The scream I heard that night—the night I arrived— never came from Trode."

"That," said Vallence in a voice from which all expression was gone, "that chanced to be the night when that unfortunate sailor was seen for the last time."

"I've thought of that, too," Roger returned grimly. "And there was the other fellow—the chap who came here—who told us how Garrow had offered him hospitality on very curious terms. Mightn't be true—but the man rang true. What does it all boil down to? That Garrow has a curious kink—a hobby for murdering tramps?"

A hand closed on Roger's wrist and tightened.

"We mustn't say that!"

"And I wouldn't—except here. But I've thought it. What of you, Mr. Vallence?"

"My dear fellow, I positively decline to answer. And now let us go across to the house. You have a few minutes to spare I am sure."

Roger said that he had and they both rose. But before they had left the church Vallence plucked at his sleeve.

"I must ask you now. I shall refer to none of our conversation outside, in case—you understand?"

"Yes."

"Have you seen *him* since those dreadful minutes in the library last night?"

"Him? No."

"Will it be all right? Can you face him as if nothing had happened?"

"Yes, I think so. I daresay he knows already. He seems to find out most things."

"Yes, but not everything. And Trode—or the Voice speaking within Trode—couldn't tell him then. Someone—something—was looking after you."

CHAPTER XXI
FATHER ROWLINSON

Marjory laid aside a book as Roger entered the drawing-room alone. Words belied action for she smiled, held out her arms to him and said:

"Don't come hear me. I'm 'catching'."

Her cheeks were a little paler and her eyes a little brighter than usual.

"I didn't know hay fever was catching," he said, going to her.

"I'm not sure either. And I'm not sure if it's hay fever." There was a pause. "Whatever it is, I'm afraid you've caught it. And now you'll give it to Dr. Garrow; and you won't be popular."

"I don't kiss Dr. Garrow—much," said Roger laughing. "Anyhow, a necromancer with hay fever would be rather a novelty."

"Ssh! He may be listening."

Roger sat down beside her and stared.

"Now what on earth made you say that?" he asked. "I don't know. I could believe anything of that man."

"So could I—almost. Well, darling! Repented yet?"

"What of?"

"It would be more correct," said Roger primly, "to say 'Of what?' Marrying me, I mean."
"But I haven't—yet."

"But you've promised to; and since you always keep your word it comes to very much the same thing. Do you love me as much as you did yesterday?"

"No," said Marjory laughing. "One doesn't love people nearly so much when one's got a beastly cold."

"It was hay fever just now. Give me another chance of catching some hay fever and then I shan't feel so disappointed."

"Yes, but I caught mine first and I should have to wait about a week for you to get over yours."

"Always thinking of yourself," said Roger severely. "I'm willing to chance it if you are."

Marjory quickly but gently repulsed him and looked in the direction of the door, t "That," she said, "is Father's cough."

"Of the warning—or churchyard—variety. Well, he needn't—"

The door was opening slowly and Marjory called out: "Oh, come in! There is nothing here that a married clergyman need fear to see."

Her farther, entering, frowned and smiled.

"My dear!" he said in-mild reproof and turned his smile almost apologetically upon Roger. "I've just found a telegram. It must have come while I was over in the church. There it was—on top of the visiting cards in the bowl in the hall. I might have missed it altogether. Guess who it's from."

"Well," said Marjory pertly, "I expect it's from one of the few hundred people you know. Or else it's from a stranger."

"It's from neither. It's from Rowlinson. He's not a stranger, but nobody will ever know Rowlinson. He's coming down this way and wants to know if he can break his journey and come to lunch. As he's already on board an express train—he handed this in at the station —it would be rather difficult to say No, even if one wanted to. That's Rowlinson all over."

He paused and turned to Roger.

"Ever heard of Father Rowlinson?"

Roger shook his head.

"No, I can't say I have. R.C. is he?"

"Yes. He went over a few years back. We were at college together. Of course we've had to agree to differ over certain matters, but he's an awfully nice fellow. I want you to meet him, Roger. There's a special reason. I—do you know I'd been thinking of writing to him? I suppose you couldn't manage to stay to lunch?"

"Well—" began Roger doubtfully.

"I know. I understand. Well, look here, you'll be coming this afternoon? All right; well, I'll hold him until then. Lock him in the bathroom if necessary. But it won't be—when he hears. You don't mind if I tell him —eh?"

"Oh!" said Roger, and thought for a moment.

The Rev. Vallence lowered an eyelid.

"I shall be showing him over the church, of course. He is interested in old churches."

Roger understood and smiled.

"Oh, that's all right," he said. "Yes, I'd like' to meet him, thanks. I suppose he won't by any chance think I'm daft?"

"If he does he'll have to think that all of us are."

Roger took his leave and went. To his relief he saw nothing of Dr. Garrow on his return, nor did Trode convey any message from him during the forenoon nor at lunch nor afterwards. The question: "Does he know where I was last night?" remained unanswered for the time. While Roger was sitting down to lunch, Vallence, looking out through one of the front windows, beheld a gaunt, upright figure in black, about six feet four inches in height, striding up the drive and swinging a large portmanteau as if it were an attache case. He ran round to the front door.

Father Rowlinson had the face and figure of a man who would have been easy to caricature. The face was a little like that of the traditional Sherlock Holmes, still more like that of a mediaeval saint much given to fasting. The lank, ungainly limbs made sharp angles as he moved them. One almost expected the knees to break through the trousers, the elbows to burst through the sleeves. Yet withal the man was no figure of fun, and when he smiled—as indeed he often did—the bleak austerity of his face remained.

Vallence never knew exactly to what extent the other's looks belied him. Rowlinson, he knew, was no anchorite. He liked a glass of wine. He could listen appreciatively to a good story and cap it with one of his own. He was charitable in speech and act. Yet the iron was there. Gentleness arid uncompromising hardness dwelt together in the same soul in strange and complex union.

"Hullo, old man."

"Hullo, my dear fellow."

The two clerics had greeted on the steps, and Vallence made an attempt to take the suit case.

"No, let me have it and tell me where to throw it. It would break the arm of a soft-living man, and I've hefted it from the station. Why, I don't know, since I'm going back almost straight away and might have left it in the cloakroom. But I didn't think of that until I got half way here, and then it wasn't worthwhile. There's a lesson in that somewhere."

And Father Rowlinson, having talked his way into the house, dumped his bag with a sigh of relief. Then, straightening his back, he made courteous inquiries after the family.

The Vicar proceeded to answer him, while piloting him into the study by the sharp crook of an arm.

"And my daughter Marjory—she's a trifle sorry for herself with hay fever at the moment—has just become engaged," he concluded.

"Well, well, well," said the Priest, sitting. He offered no congratulations, but waited to hear more. Vallence, however, turned the subject for the while by asking what brought him to that part of the world.

"I'm finishing a holiday. I was sworn to come and see you some day. So I made a bit of a detour on my way back. Your daughter going to be married, did you say? Who is hi?"

"An awfully nice fellow named Moorlock, a school friend of my son. At present he's secretary, librarian and so forth to a rather queer neighbour of ours, a Dr. Garrow."

As he pronounced the name the Vicar glanced swiftly at the priest. That quick interrogative look was rewarded. He saw the pale, thin face lift with a start. "Not Dr. Eustace Roderick Garrow?"

"Yes. I think that's his full name. Why?"

There was a moment's silence.

"My God!" said the priest drearily and even prayerfully.

Vallence rose.

"Do you mind coming over into the church?" he said. "There's something I want to tell you, and I'd rather tell you there."

"Yes," said the priest," and I know why."

They went out bare-headed and covered half the distance to the church in silence.

"It's a fine old church," said the Vicar, clearing his throat, "but I'm afraid it looks better outside than in."

"Ye-es," said Father Rowlingson gently. "Pre-reformation, I see."

The Vicar glanced sidelong at him and saw for a moment a faint smile flicker on the cadaverous face. Then—since he was grateful for any cause to laugh— he burst out laughing.

"I shall owe you a dig for that," he said.

They entered and sat together in a pew in the rear of the nave and close to the font. Vallence pushed a hassock away from under his feet and turned to the man sitting beside him.

"What do you know about Garrow?" he asked in an undertone.

"A great deal more, my dear fellow, than I intend to to tell you."

"Anything to do with—Satanism?"

"Satanism? Now that's a very odd word."

"You know what I mean. I'm going to tell you a few things presently. Would you say that the young man was in danger in that house?"

"I should say in grave danger."

"To body or soul?"

"I should say to both. It depends on himself."

The Vicar fidgeted.

"Your people believe in Possession, do they not?"

"Do not yours? There are sufficient cases in the New Testament."

"Have you ever met a case?"

"Ever met? Unfortunately I have met a great many. A number of so-called lunatics are possessed. Others walk abroad and are able to hide the Beast."

Vallence nodded once or twice.

"You practise exorcism, do you not?"

"The Church does, I don't. It is a subject which very few of us could tell you anything about—and I am not one of the very few. The power of exorcism is given us at ordination—and taken away at the same time. The reason, I suppose, is to prevent silly people with a disposition to sin from running to their parish priest and demanding to be exorcised. The power of exorcism is, however, restored again to one priest in every diocese. Nobody knows who retains it but the man himself, the bishop and the bishop's secretary. If a case came my way I should have to inform the bishop, and he would take steps to deaL with it if the victim—or those in charge of the victim—were willing. O'Flynn, my assistant, may be the diocesan exorcist for all I know. And if he isn't, I may be the man for all he knows."

The Rev. Vallence lowered his voice.

"Supposing something—something went wrong with poor Roger, would you help?"

"Certainly. I'd write to our bishop here—if you'd corroborate. I am certain he would help. Let me see, that would be the Bishop of Portsmouth. All we diversely- believing Christians must stand shoulder to shoulder when fighting—*that.* And now will you kindly tell me all that's been happening here?"

"I'll tell you all that I know," said Vallence, "and I expect you have read one or two extraordinary items of news concerning the happenings around here."

He lowered his voice and proceeded to tell as much as he knew of the story and of Roger's experiences. The other listened silently and gloomily.

"So," he concluded, "what do you make of it?"

"Just Horror," the priest answered sadly. "Just sheer dreadful Horror."

"Ah, and now—and now won't you tell me what you know of Garrow?"

Father Rowlinson hesitated.

"I have heard a great deal," he said quietly, "but I must not slander. I must not speak ill without certain knowledge. I will tell you one thing—and one thing only. There was a man of that name about to be tried in Madrid for Satanism. A revolution broke out and saved him."

"This last revolution, you mean?"

"No. I am bad at dates. This one occurred in the eighteen-thirties or early forties."

Vallence started violently and uttered a sharp cry.

"It can't be the same man!"

"Forgive me, but you are wrong. I don't say that it is the same man—but I say that it can be."

"That would make him to be—How has he kept himself alive?"

"There are ways and means—if a man seek them from the Enemy. But the end must come in time—the dire, unthinkable end."

"What did you think of the case of the Stolen Body? Thurley's body, I mean? You must have read of it." The priest answered the question with another. "What did you think of Thurley, my friend?"

"A brilliant man. An amazingly brilliant man. But in his declining years—" Vallence paused and shrugged. "You know which way genius so often turns."

"Yes, and I know what common men like us so often think of genius."

"He told me that he had a secret which would die with him for the good of mankind. Garrow told Roger that he knew what it was—although the two were not on speaking terms. Roger told me that Garrow had told him, laughing, that the old man thought he was an alchemist."

"Ah!"

Vallence eyed him narrowly.

"Come now! Is it because you are in my church that you won't smile?"

"Not altogether."

Vallence continued to stare.

"You don't believe that alchemy is a scientific possibility, surely?"

"No, I don't. And I don't believe the Miracles were scientific possibilities."

"Well, we can agree there. They were not, but we believe they happened. None the less, I cannot imagine God permitting one of His creatures to become a sort of Midas."

"Not God, perhaps," said the priest, smiling. "But our scepticism does not matter. We may not believe it possible; but others may believe. And that, after all, may not have been his supposed secret."

"Can you think why his body was stolen?"

The gaunt priest slowly inclined his head.

"Oh, yes. And I think I know who has it? But I must not say."

"Then what do you really think about it all?"

Father Rowlinson hesitated.

"If one sought infernal aid—I have heard of such things—it might be possible to restore life for a little while. I say it might be—through the fusion of another soul. Then, if he had a secret, he could be made to blurt it."

"How?"

" *'Methinks thou speak'st but on the rack, Where men enforced do say anything.'* That's in *'The Merchant of Venice,'* isn't it? Anyhow, the method would apply today. Suppose you could, bring your dead man to life for a while—so that his body and members could feel—and then stick his hand on a red-hot coal—he would probably become rapidly confidential about his closest secrets."

Vallence uttered a short gasp. His companion met his gaze and held it for a moment.

"You can't think—you don't think—that that is what is happening, or going to happen?"

"I think," the priest returned gently, "that you should get your young friend out of that house as soon as possible. It cannot be a healthy house."

"I know. He is in danger. I feel that. We all feel it. And he knows. But he means to stay. He seems determined to find out everything and then—if the seemingly impossible is true—to fight the Powers of Darkness. Poor Roger, so strong among men, so puny against that man and his dreadful allies."

"Why, then," said Father Rowlinson, "he is a very brave man, and so I shall pray for him. And, if you will permit it, I will have a little private word with him this afternoon. Nothing to make him think me an old lunatic—at least, so I hope. I have heard of cases—well, not similar, but yet in their different ways analogous."

He rose slowly and stepped carefully over a hassock. "And now, if I may, I will walk around your beautiful church. Oh yes, it's beautiful still. You could do with some more stained glass. I suppose all the old stuff went in the seventeenth century—when the Puritans were throwing stones. If I were you, I shouldn't mind begging for my beautiful church. Who is the richest person in the parish?"

Vallence smiled wryly, biting his lip.

"Need you ask me that?" he said.

Father Rowlinson threw up his hands. A look of half-humorous apology instantly crossed his face.

"Oh!" he exclaimed. "I ought to have known! My dear fellow! I am so awfully sorry."

CHAPTER XXII
FATHER ROWLINSON SPEAKS

Roger, shown into the Vicarage drawing-room at about twenty minutes to four that afternoon, found Marjory smoking a cigarette and strumming the piano. She dropped her hands and turned as he went over to her.

"Well, darling," he greeted her, "and how are you feeling now?"

"Pretty—ahem. No, don't kiss me."

"You forget that I kissed you this morning, so if I'm going to catch anything I've caught it already. I tried to get you some grapes, but that baffled the resources of our local shop. They asked me if a tin of pineapple would do. Now suppose you come over to the chesterfield and lay your head on my shoulder and tell me all about your temperature."

Marjory gently and deftly pulled his nose as he bent over her.

"Not now," she said. "Your presence is urgently desired elsewhere. Father—my father, I mean—and Father Rowlinson are waiting for you."

"Where?"

"Over in the church. Father Rowlinson wants to meet you there, and not elsewhere for the present. I don't quite know why."

"I think I do," said Roger.

"Well, be a good lad and run along. Don't keep them waiting. I shall see you at tea-time."

He kissed her again and went. The church door stood open and the Vicar and his guest were standing talking together at the bottom of the central aisle.

The Vicar looked round, smiled and spoke in a whisper. "Oh, Roger, let me introduce you to Father Rowlinson. I have told you a little about him, I have told him a great deal about you." The tall, gaunt priest looked apparaisingly at Roger as he inclined his head.

"And now," said Vallence, "I am going to leave you two together."

"There is no need for you to go," said Father Rowlinson.

"Forgive me, but I think there is. A confidential talk between three takes longer and is less intimate than a confidential chat between two. So I will leave you to it. I will have tea kept waiting until I see you again."

He went. As the latch of the door clicked behind him Roger, looking after him, felt a gentle touch on his arm.

"Shall we make ourselves comfortable and sit in one of the pews?" Father Rowlinson suggested. "We are to have a confidential talk—if you will honour me with your confidence. It is a pity that it must be here, for it prevents us from smoking. However, I have another solace."

He produced an enormous snuff box which he opened and 6ffered to Roger, who smilingly declined. Father Rowlinson then helped himself to two heaped-up pinches, dabbed with an enormous red handkerchief, smiled and said:

"I gave it up once during Lent, but never again. My housekeeper complained about my temper. Now let's sit down. I don't think we can be *overheard* here. I understand from my old friend Vallence that you are willing to give me your confidence.' In return I may be able to help, or at least advise you."

"About Garrow?"

"Yes. Tell me the whole story as you would put it down in a book. I won't interrupt. I'll save all my questions until the end."

“I think,” said Roger, “that I shall do most of the questioning.”

“Well, then, I will answer if I can.”

It was Roger indeed who subsequently did most of the questioning. He told his tale concisely and in detail. Now and again he looked at the stern, sad face beside him, but it remained grave, impassive and inscrutable.

“Well, Father Rowlinson,” he said at last, “I think that is all I can possibly tell you. If I have left out anything at all I am sure it is nothing of any importance. And now, you have had some experience in these matters—”

“I have had no first-hand experience of anything like this. But I have learned certain things.”

“What do you make of it all?”

“My dear sir, you put me in a quandary. There are things that one scarcely likes to say—even to an intimate. You and I are meeting for the first time. Oh, well, I have had a lot of experience of the confessional. I am not afraid of hearing or using unminced words. But, my dear sir, I don’t want you to go away saying— or at least thinking—that the old priest who talked to you was mad.”

“It was what I was afraid you would think about me,” said Roger, smiling.

Father Rowlinson nodded twice and smiled faintly.

“Well, first of all, that unspeakable man is a Satanist. He is able to practice that which—for want of a better name—we will call the Black Art. He can see within limits where he wishes to see—in the crystal. I say ‘within limits’ because I do not think he can see us here. He has this man Trode completely under his control. He can put Trode into a trance and in that trance some devil from the pit takes command. Between them they have murdered at least two men—”

“But why?”

“Listen, my friend. That poor man Thurley died with a secret—or so it was supposed. Your Dr. Garrow desires it. He has the body. The body was stolen out of its grave by his orders. One of the men who stole it got drunk and became a danger, so he was murdered. Who did it? I think I can answer. Trode. *You* didn’t hear Trode scream out that night. Dr. Garrow did. Then you heard Dr. Garrow talking—not merely to a deaf man, but to a man who wasn’t there. That was Trode’s alibi.

“What lies behind it all? I will try to tell you what I think. It is possible, or alleged to be possible, to revive a dead man—for at least a short period—by an odious and repulsive process. It entails human sacrifice. The blood and breath of a dying man are needed. There are certain rites with which I am not conversant and which, I am informed, are too horrible to be discussed.

"It seems to me that that unspeakable person has tried once or twice and failed. Perhaps he had got a sigh and a choked breath and a muttered word, but nothing more. He wants more. He wants the secret that died with Thurley. If he can transfuse life into Thurley for more than a few seconds the secret may become his. He will use torture."

Roger shuddered and looked straight down the aisle.

"Why hasn't he—tried to murder me?" he asked jerkily.

"That may have been his original intention, I don't know. But your knowing the Vallences made things extremely awkward for him. Again, it may suit him to have about the house a man of integrity who knows nothing of what is going on. Besides, he hinted to you pretty broadly that he was in danger. He knows he may need your strong right arm, my friend." Roger nodded again.

"Yes," he said, "but in what circumstance?"

The priest dropped his voice to a whisper.

"Has it not occurred to you," he breathed jerkily, "that it might—be dangerous—to bring a body to life—and then find it—possessed by a devil?"

There was a spell of silence. Roger turned a pale, bewildered face on his companion.

"What would you do," he asked slowly, "if you were I?"

Father Rowlinson answered him simply and humbly.

"I had rather you did not press me. God help me, I am not a brave man. My advice to you—the advice I feel bound to give you—is to leave that house at once."

"But if murder has been done?"

"You are not a policeman. You are the friend of an old and dear friend of mine, affianced to his daughter."

"Suppose I were not? Suppose you had never heard of me before we had this talk?"

"Oh, then I should say God bless you—and God help you."

"If that man—whose money I am taking, and I'm not too proud of it—is a murderer and worse, I am going to do my best to finish him. If it came to a fight, I could kill both Trode and him with my two hands. But he has command of other powers. What can I do if a crisis comes? I can take no holy thing into the house without his being aware of it and stealing it from me."

"All that you can do is to have faith and cry out on God. Remember always that He is stronger than the Enemy. The Enemy is powerful; He Is omnipotent. Keep that thought always in your heart. Challenge when the time comes, in God's Name, and then I think you need not fear the raging devil which may be unleashed when life returns to the poor carcase which he has concealed."

There was another pause.

"Thank you, Father Rowlinson," said Roger at last.

"You have been very kind. I—"

He came awkwardly to a pause and Father Rowlinson suddenly laughed.

"Bless the boy's heart! He wants to ask me to pray for him, and doesn't like to. Well, so I will. And take my blessing, too." Grey eyes twinkled suddenly. "You may doubt its efficacy, but you would have to admit that it cannot possibly harm you. And now I will tell you what I shall do. There is a certain man at Scotland Yard—one of the big men. He used to come to my church before he was transferred. Quite a good-living man—for a policeman. At least, I managed to get him to his duties about twice a year. I'll try to get hold of him, and if I can drag him inside a church I'll tell him. That house and that man need watching. If only there were evidence enough to obtain a search-warrant! But that will come in time."

In speaking the last words he rose slowly and touched Roger on the shoulder.

"Come along," he said. "A certain young woman will be getting impatient."

Inside the Vicarage they separated for a while. Roger went to join Marjory in the drawing-room; the priest turned towards the Vicar's study. The Rev. Vallence looked up.

"Well?" he said.

Father Rowlinson shrugged his shoulders.

"I've heard it all," he said. "It's pretty bad, you know."

"Yes," said Vallence dully. "Did you try to get him to leave?"

"My dear fellow, there was once a saint called George. I don't know what sort of dragon it was that he faced. I imagine—since legends have a way of getting distorted —that it was an evil spirit, or some being possessed of one. Anyhow, had I lived at that time I should not have tried to deter St. George from facing it."

Marjory smiled at Roger as he entered the drawing room.

"Well," she said, "have you had a nice talk?"

Roger grimaced.

"No," he replied, "I haven't. He's an awfully decent chap, though. I've come in for a nice talk with you, for a change."

He sat beside her and slipped an arm about her waist. "Have you any more spare germs to give away?"

CHAPTER XXIII
THE HORROR BENEATH THE FLOOR

Dr. Garrow did not come down to dinner that night; and Roger did not care to ask Trode if his master were in or out. Instinct warned him that the fewer questions he asked Trode the better.

On the whole, he was glad to be relieved of Dr. Garrow's company. He could not rid himself of the thought that Garrow would have at least an inkling as to the company he had been keeping that afternoon; and although he might know nothing more he was capable ot surmising a great deal.

He had nearly finished dinner when a thought occurred to him. Trode in his position could neither permit nor forbid an expressed intention. He took out a notebook and scribbled hastily—

"If Dr. Garrow wants me between now and ten o'clock I shall be somewhere in the gardens—so do not lock me out." Trode read, seemed to hesitate and then bowed slightly. Roger watched him closely and thought he saw the least shadow cross the man's face. But it was gone on the instant. Roger, knowing that look, smiled to himself. It was the facial expression of the underling who would, but dares not, raise an objection.

A few minutes later, having provided himself with cigarettes and matches, Roger walked out. The evening was still light, and indeed it would be hardly dark by the time he had mentioned for his return.

In all the weeks he had been with Dr. Garrow he had riot walked in those gardens more than three or four times, and with this thought in his mind he laughed at his own choice of a word. Gardens? If these were gardens, it was a garden in which Ishmael the outcast wandered.

Swinburne's *"Forsaken Carden"* was somewhere on the horizon of his memory and he tried to recollect a line or two.

"Not a breath of the time that has been hovers In the air now soft with a summer to be..."

But that was not' entirely apt, although the ruined beds and hayfield lawns looked like a building site disdained by builders. There were two decayed summerhouses and three arbours, and these conveyed the suggestion that the house had once been owned by normal and probably kindly people who had loved their grounds.

Roger paused at the choked-up entrance to an arbour and pushed aside ungainly masses of drooping honeysuckle and clinging creeper. Then he looked around for a stick and presently sent aside a flimsy barrier of spiders' webs and dangling strings of grime. Inside there was a rustic bench and a shapeless rustic table. Roger sat on the bench, drew his cigarettes out on to the table, and sat looking out and across the grass through little wind-stirred loopholes in the foliage.

He would, he supposed, afterwards find his clothes full of spiders, earwigs and other such denizens of neglected arbours; but he did not greatly mind. He was free for the while of the hellish atmosphere of the house he had just left. That it was hellish he no longer doubted, since now he felt by contrast this serenity. As the minutes passed and the light outside gently waned he felt more and more unwilling to return indoors. He had heard of soldiers in shell-proof dugouts who felt a cold, humiliating reluctance to climb out of safety into the open trench, even when all was quiet. Dugout disease he had heard that it was called. He began to think that he could understand.

There was a summerhouse opposite him, across the waste which had once been a lawn; and he fell to wondering if he would not have done better to choose it rather than his present insect-haunted retreat. The thought, joined with that of the possibility of crossing over to it, kept his gaze on the little round open-fronted structure—or of as much of it as he could see through the leafy barrier before him. Thus he was looking straight across in that direction when Trode came into view, making upon it—as indeed he was almost compelled to do—by a flanking movement.

Trode carried a small tray. On it, as Roger at that distance surmised more than he saw, was a bottle, a glass and a syphon. Trode had come out to give him a whisky and soda, and this seemed very kind and thoughtful of Trode.

This, at least, Roger would have thought of any other servant, but of Trode he was not so sure. He was less sure than ever a few moments later. Trode was moving quite noiselessly. He was quite obviously creeping. He stopped altogether once, and his free hand moved up to steady something on the tray which possibly had rattled. Roger smiled and went on watching him.

There is a peculiar kind of satisfaction—reminiscent of childhood and games of hide-and-seek—in lying concealed and watching the searcher at his work. Trode's approach to the summerhouse grew slower as the distance lessened. Head bent forward, he took one slow step at a time until at last he had a view of the empty space within.

He stood poised for a moment,, his body leaning over the tray and his head protruding around the angle of the entrance. Then he drew himself up, turned in the direction of the arbour in which Roger was sitting, and came rustling carelessly through the grass, all the former and —it seemed—unnecessary caution gone.

He looked in, saw Roger, brushed his way through the honeysuckle and creeper and, with a faint, obliging smile on his livid face, set down the tray. Roger let the man read his lips.

"Thank you very much indeed, Trode. That's very kind of you."

Trode smiled again, bowed, turned and went. Roger spoke to him aloud behind his back, getting a grim and unashamed satisfaction out of the advantage.

"You devil! You didn't want me in that place opposite! Why not?"

Standing at the entrance to the arbour he watched Trode vanish within doors. He was meanwhile making a mathematical calculation. Could he sprint across the lawn—if still it could be called that—before Trode could get to any window within doors from which he could spy? Once in the summer-house opposite, Roger would be as free from observation as before. Almost on the instant he saw that he could make the distance easily; and next moment he had broken cover.

The little wooden structure was sexangular and a fixed bench ran round five of its sides. Apart from this it was devoid of furniture. The floor was bare, with dust and dried mud stains on the grey and dingy boards.

Roger, looking about him and frowning, fell to wondering why Trode, having seemed to suspect that he was there, should have gone to such pains to spy upon him. Here was nothing to reward a prying eye. And then his own prying eye caught a faint gleam on the floor in the fading light. He bent over the little round and faintly shining disc and saw that it was a nail head driven in flush with the boards.

There was nothing remarkable in this at first thought. All the boards were nailed. Yes, and all the other nails were rusty veterans. Roger, chin in hand, stood wondering what this tiny discovery meant.

Strange that on premises where the out buildings were all in a state of neglected decay, somebody should have troubled to drive *one new nail* into a board. Then fast upon him came memories of his own very slight experiences of wood and nails.

If one removes nails carefully they may be used again. A bent one must be replaced. He looked down closely at the boards. They were all flush, but here and there, he thought he could discern the marks of scars. He rubbed one of these scars with his thumb, and the dirt— evidently of recent accumulation—came away quite readily showing clean, pale wood. Now all was so far clear to him. The boards, or at least some of them, had quite recently been taken up and nailed down again. One nail had broken, or become too bent to be used a second time. A new one had been pressed into service, and this recruit in a company of seasoned veterans had made the betrayal.

Roger had in his pocket a knife containing many extra fittings; indeed, the kind of knife beloved of schoolboys.

There was nothing in it specially designed for taking nails out of boards, but of the half dozen fittings he hoped to find something that would do.

He found the small blade as useful as anything. The nails in old and dry wood were loose. He needed to prize them up only so far as was necessary to get the least finger grip and they came up with very little resistance. He put them aside carefully one by one, reflecting that subsequently his own heel would make an effective and noiseless hammer.

The first board came up and revealed a dark cavity from which white dust came flying like a cloud of minute insects suddenly freed. Mingled odours rose with it: the smell of lime and a stench putrescent and sickening. He struck a match and looked down to see a heap of sacking, wet and rotting and lime-stained.

He peered nearer, his nose wrinkled in disgust; then he started back, a cry upon his lips and sudden nausea in this throat.

"Oh, my God!" he heard his own voice exclaim.

For that which protruded from the sacking, mummified, lime-stained and half skeleton, was the claw-fingered hand of a man; and Roger knew that he looked down not merely on death but on bloody murder.

He stooped in the one attitude for a long half-minute, taking a grip on himself. His instinct was to rush' straight for the police, restraint counselled otherwise. Policemen require finding in country places. If he exhibited horror and excitement the body would not be there when the police came to search. It meant spending just one more night in that house of damnation and, if he met Garrow trying to appear as if nothing untoward had happened. Afterwards? Well, it remained to be seen if Garrow and Trode—either or both—would suffer the penalty of the law. The mere discovery of the body was no proof of their guilt. No doubt, Dr. Garrow—with unholy wisdom to guide him—would have his answer ready. Probably too he had counted on the possibility of discovery, remote as it may have seemed to him, and—as in chess—thought several moves ahead.

As he replaced the boards, carefully treading down the nails, which he forced back without much difficulty into the holes from which they had been wrenched, Roger made up his mind. He decided to go back to the house and straight to his room, at the same time hoping and praying that Dr. Garrow would not insist on seeing him that night.

If Dr. Garrow insisted, it might be dangerous for him indeed. He had received a severe shock and he supposed that he must show it. His mere looks might betray his knowledge. Then?

Well, he was more than a match for Garrow and Trode combined if it came to a battle with nature's weapons; but the heavyweight champion of the world is no match for a child—if the child has a five-shilling second-hand pistol.

It was early twilight when he returned to the house, entered the hall and got safely upstairs to his room without encountering Garrow or Trode. He went straight to the dressing-table and looked at himself in the glass.

" 'I met Murder on my way'," he quoted to himself. "Yes, and I damned well look like it! A nice, easy job. Good salary. Well, somebody else can damned well have it tomorrow—for so long as it lasts. Now for God's sake let me try to look like myself. That hell-hound may come prying round at any moment."

Even while the thought was passing he heard a step outside the, door; then a knock. Roger heard himself say: "Yes?" The mellow voice of Dr. Garrow responded as the door was pushed open.

"Oh, you're here, are you? I did not see you at dinner because—" He stopped himself abruptly to peer into Roger's face. "Why," he said gently, "you do not seem to be looking very well. Let me feel your pulse."

"No," said Roger sharply, and drew back.

"Oh, very well, very well." Dr. Garrow smiled and uttered his characteristic chirrup. "I know exactly what you have been doing."

Roger responded with one blunt word: "What?"

His hands were behind him and he kept them there; but now he had unclasped them and they became fists. The air in his nostrils and about his ears seemed to be tingling and throbbing with suspense.

Slightly to Roger's surprise, and greatly to his relief. Dr. Garrow sat down. His smiling air, or archness—which might have been the cloak of strong emotion, violent and sinister—never for a moment left him.

"You saw a certain lady this afternoon and found her stricken by one of the seventy or eighty ailments which the ignorant know no better than to call by one name— Influenza." He waited to hear Roger exclaim; and for once he misunderstood the cause.

"I have previously given you exhibitions of this small gift of mine. Well, let me proceed. The lady, very properly, urged you to keep at a respectful distance. You, however, in a foolish but otherwise enviable condition, thought otherwise. Well; well, you pay the penalty. You will no doubt derive some consolation when you reflect on the source from which the germs came; but if I were you I should not keep them nor encourage them- to multiply any longer than I could possibly help. Let me get you some quinine."

Roger smiled. Almost he could hear his heart singing for relief.

"No—no, thank you," he stammered. "I hate the stuff."

"Preferring the ailment to the remedy," said Garrow, with his gentle smile. "I suggest a pleasanter alternative, and almost as efficacious. I have some excellent liqueur whisky which you have not yet tried. You had better remain here, since you are not well, and I will go and get you a glass."

Roger, anxious only to be rid of him, could hardly find a word to say. Garrow left him—to fume and fidget for the- next five minutes—until he returned with a tray on which there was a tumbler half full of pale neat spirit.

"It is undiluted," he said. "A liqueur, as I told you; and something over proof. But it will not hurt you, and you will find it as soft as milk to the palate."

Roger took the glass from him and thanked him. There was a sudden hiatus in talk and action.

"Go on," said Dr. Garrow, laughing softly. "Drink it." Those who refused a glass of wine with the Borgias—when Death was mixed with it—received instead cold steel in the back upon their homeward way. Now, it seemed, was the time for inspired acting.

"I'll drink it in bed," said Roger casually and without a false note in his voice. "Then I can settle straight down to sleep."

He watched Dr. Garrow as he spoke. Was there the least shadow on his face? If so, it was the merest ghost of shade. -In this subtle duel between them neither must appear aware that the duel existed. Garrow, on his side, dared not risk being too importunate.

"Oh, as you please, as you please," he said lightly. "Let me know tomorrow what you think of it. I hope you will be your own self again by tomorrow. And so Good-night."

"Good-night," echoed Roger.

CHAPTER XXIV
FRIENDS IN NEED

Left alone, Roger picked up the glass of whisky. He savoured it with a wrinkled, suspicious nose. He could detect nothing wrong with it, his jangled nerves asked for it, yet he put it by and looked at it.

The story of Dr. Johnson and the too hot potato—"Madam, a fool would have swallowed that"—carried into his mind without begging the semblance of a smile. He had eaten and drunk enough in that house without the least fear or suspicion of poison. If that thought were to darken his mind, he must leave at once or starve. Rut that Inner Voice—which is so often wrong yet still continues to deserve attention—was telling him insistently not to touch that glass of whisky.

The memory of that withered, lime-eaten hand protruding from under the sacks, was no doubt the cause of his reluctance to drink. Paradoxically, it was also the cause of his need for stimulant. Roger considered the matter, frowning.

On the whole, perhaps, this was where one should play for safety. He walked over to the slop-pail and paused. No, that would not do. Trode probably had a nose like a bloodhound's to compensate for his loss of hearing, and the act would be detected and reported to Dr. Garrow.

On the dressing-table stood a brilliantine bottle nearly empty, containing indeed only enough for one moderate application. Roger did not waste it. Then, having brushed and combed his hair, he carefully rinsed out the bottle. It just sufficed to hold the whisky. He corked it carefully and slipped it into a pocket.

"Just out of curiosity," he thought, "there couldn't be any harm in letting a chemist have a look at this."

Roger tried to quieten his mind by reading for half an hour. Then he climbed into bed and tried to will himself to sleep.

He succeeded at last, but afterwards he could have wished it otherwise. He dreamed of looking down through a hole in the floor through which the dust of lime was rising—looking down through the dust to a heap of lime beneath, from which protruded the mummified claw of a hand.

As he watched, the hand moved and he knew that in a moment the occupant of that burning bed would rise up and reveal all of himself. Then he woke with a start, a scream ringing in his ears.

At first he was not at all sure, as he sat up in bed choking and weak with horror, if the scream were part of the nightmare. It had some indescribable quality of detachment, or sounded in the dream as if it- came from a distance. It had seemed to have nothing to do with that lime-eaten body under the summer-house floor.

Awake he found himself weak with terror. His manhood, the traditions of his kind, urged him to rise and go out and see if there were anything amiss in the house. He might be told that it was only Trode—and it *might* be Trode. But he knew what held him and he knew the meaning of his dry throat and sweating hands. He was afraid. Roger Moorlock was afraid, and the thought of that alone brought savage tears to his eyes.

After some moments of internal combat he felt the floor under his feet. The soul of Roger-was driving his body, whipping it like a flagging horse. He got into clothes and shoes and crept outside and along to the head of the stairs.

The house was quiet enough now—if it had ever been disturbed. On silent feet Roger went down into the hall. At first everything seemed normal. A little light from the luminous skies filtered through the windows, and in one of these faint beams he saw something shape-.less and unfamiliar lying on the floor. He scarcely guessed what it was before his hand encountered it, and then the sense of touch told him that which was presently confirmed by sight. It was an old and battered felt hat.

Roger went quickly and quietly upstairs with his find. In the light of his bedroom he examined it. The hat had once been brown; it was now almost green. The lining was gone and the crown discoloured by sweat. In the tattered leather just under the brim a name was faintly legible,' written in ink by a painstaking, uneducated hand.

"P. Dolan"—or was it "Dalan"? Probably the former. And what was it doing on the floor of the hall? It certainly was not his own. It was almost farcical to think that at some time Garrow might have borrowed it. And Trode was no more likely than his master to crown himself with a wreck which was fit only for topping a scarecrow."

"There's been bloody murder here again tonight," he thought wildly. "Yes, it's devils' work. Those two padres know what they are saying. Well, tomorrow I begin to act. I want this dirty old hat as evidence. The filthy thing goes under my pillow and if one of those hell-begotten swine comes in and tries to get it I'll tear out his blasted wind-pipe and trample on it."

The silent outburst did him good. He wrapped the unsavoury headgear in many layers of paper—"lest," he thought grimly, "something escapes from it"—'and thrust it under the pillow upon which he presently laid his own head.

He woke with the events of the previous night crowding back into his mind. Trode was in the room setting down his tea-tray. Trode, turning to glance at him, saw him awake, and it seemed to Roger that he saw sudden surprise on the man's face. The look was smoothed out immediately afterwards as the man inclined his head in greeting. Roger too nodded Good morning.

It was Trode's custom to efface himself immediately he had brought in the tea. This morning he departed from it. He drew notebook find pencil from a pocket and scribbled hastily on a leaf which he presently tore out and handed to Roger.

"Excuse me sir but you haven't seen a old hat of mine soft felt which I wares sometimes in the gardin I cant find it nowheres and I like that old hat if you know what I mean!' Roger was broad awake now. He looked at the man and lied brazenly with a gesture. As he shook his head his elbow rested on the pillow under which the crumpled hat was lying.

Trode seemed motionless. He shook his own head, as one would say interrogatively, "No?" Then he went quietly from the room, leaving Roger to nod to himself.

Ah, but no doubt that hat was worrying them.' No doubt they had been looking for it everywhere. It had dropped off in a scuffle in the hall before the latest victim had succumbed. Possibly and even probably they had been arguing as to whether the man had worn a hat. There was a certain grim humour in the situation which won a wry smile from Roger.

The hat remained in Roger's very close keeping while he was in the house. He took it with him to the bath room. He wore it crushed flat inside the breast of his sports coat when he went down to breakfast. And after breakfast he went out before his usual time.

He went straight to the Vicarage. The Rev. Vallence was in the hall and about to go out when Roger climbed the steps. He started and laughed.

"Hullo, my dear fellow! This is early for you." He stared and laughed, but the laugh died away. "My dear boy, I don't like the look you've brought with you."

"People didn't like the look of Dante—after they thought he'd seen Hell. Could you spare a moment? Would you mind coming over to the church with me?"

"Oh!" said the Vicar, comprehendingly.

Over in the church he turned suddenly tremulous, nerves shaking a voice which sounded almost tearful;

"My dear boy, what is it now? What is it now?" and he fawned upon Roger's shoulders with his hands.

"It's murder," said Roger in a choked voice. "I've found a body. And I believe murder was done again last night."

"Found—*found* a body?"

"Buried in lime under the floor of a summer-house. And look here—here's a hat. I found it in the hall last night. But I'll tell you the whole story."

Roger did so, leaning against the back of a pew. The Vicar looked more and more aghast, but said hardly a word until the tale was told. Roger, coming to the end, took a bottle from his pocket.

"Here's the whisky he brought me last night. I don't think it's poisoned. He's no cause to harm me—unless he thinks I know too much—and besides he daren't. You live so close at hand, and he knows you could start a great deal of trouble if anything happened to me. I'm not a poor, friendless tramp.

"But I'll wager anything that the stuff's drugged. He wanted me safely unconscious while—er—something happened to the late owner of that hat. It isn't very important—the matter of the whisky, I mean—but I'd like to find out if there's anything in it."

The Vicar held out his hand for the bottle.

"I'll give it to Dr. Simpson and get him to send it up for analysis; but that will take days. Meanwhile, what is to be done about—*you* know. I mean, that poor body burning in the lime, and the man who threw the lime over it?"

"That's the trouble," said Roger. "Directly a move is taken he'll see it coming and make the counter-move. You know—I've told you—he's got his own fiendish ways of finding out things. Last night, when he saw me looking sick after what I'd found—and hence his excuse for forcing the whisky on me—he knew that I'd been to see Marjory and that Marjory was ill. How did he know that Marjory was ill? He seemed to think that it was influenza or something infections."

The Vicar shrugged his shoulders helplessly.

"He was wrong. She's much better to-day. But, as you say, how did he know at all? Now, listen to me, Roger. Once more, my dear boy—*don't* go back to that house!"

"If I don't he'll suspect that I've found out something, and the body won't be there when the police come."

"And if you were to take a policeman here and now and show it to him, the chances are that there would not be enough evidence available to arrest him on the spot. The summer-house from what you tell me is some distance from the house. Anybody might have hidden the body there in the dead of night. There's no *prima facie* case against Garrow. It might take days to assemble sufficient evidence and then, when it was complete, Garrow would be gone. And—" Vallence sank his voice—"and meanwhile, my dear Roger, something very unpleasant might happen to you."

"That's just what I've been thinking," Roger confessed laughing. "In for a penny, in for a pound, and he wouldn't stick at much. I can't do anything to defend my life until he makes a direct attempt on it—and then I might not succeed. It's like being in a duel in which the other man is allowed the first shot at any distance and at his own leisure."

Vallence hesitated and considered for a long minute. "I know what I'll do. I'll get Stillby—you remember Inspector Stillby?—on the telephone. He's on those two other cases, I suppose. Thurley's body and the murder of that poor gardener of mine. I'll tell him that there's somebody with exclusive information for him—and for him only—if he comes over at once. I'm sure he'll shelve everything else. As soon as he arrives he'll be told- that he can have that information only inside my church. I don't know what he'll think, but that's beside the point. I imagine he's more concerned with the end than the means."

He paused and laid a hand on Roger's shoulder.

"I'll get on the telephone now," he said. "Come over and see Marjory."

They left the church together. Marjory met them in the hall of the Vicarage and her father went straight past them without a word. When his back had vanished Roger took her into his arms.

"I'm so glad you're better to-day, dear."

"Yes, thanks, but—" She paused and stared and her voice rose to a cry. *"Darling!* What's the matter? You look *awful"*

She led him into the dining-room and sat beside him, drawing one of his arms around her neck. He hid his eyes against her cheek and she felt him trembling.

"What is it?" she whispered. "What is it?"

"I can't tell you now, dear," he murmured in a broken voice. "I'm not so strong as I thought. My nerves are not what I thought they were. And the strain of all that's happened in the last few weeks—"

He came to a pause and held her closer.

"But it's coming to an end now. It's coming to an end now. Thank God, it can't go on."
She had the tact to say no more, to let him rest in silence in the warmth and comfort of her near presence. Only when she heard footfalls outside the room she gently disengaged his arms and smiled meaningly at him. Her father came in.

"I've been on the telephone," he announced. "Pie—you know whom I mean—is coming over early in the afternoon. To-day, at any rate, you'd better stay to lunch."

"Oh, thank you very much." Roger uttered a laugh, thin and high-pitched, in contrast to his normal laughter.

"I'm not at all afraid—any longer—of getting the sack."

CHAPTER XXV
INSPECTOR STILLBY LEARNS

Shortly after three o'clock Roger, sitting in the drawing-room with Marjory and her Mother, heard the dinning of the electric bell at the front door. But no visitor was announced and twenty minutes passed before the Rev. Vallence opened the door and looked in. He captured Roger's gaze and made a backward motion of the head. Roger made a brief apology and went out. Vallence, his fingers still on the handle, closed it after him and spoke in a low voice.

"Come along. He's over in the church. You know whom."

"Have you told him?"

"Something—yes."

"What does he say?"

"Nothing. He just wants to see you."

Roger turned drearily towards the do6r.

"I know what it will be," he said. "He'll think I'm mad. Or else he'll—"

He checked himself. The Vicar pinched his arm and tapped his shoulder to guide him to the hall door. They walked across and entered the church together. Stillby was waiting just outside.'

"You've met before," the Vicar said simply, and withdrew a step behind Roger. Stillby, looking at Roger, nodded.

"How are you, sir? Now let's sit down and have a talk—if this gentleman will permit."

They went to sit in one of the back pews. The Vicar stood behind them, fidgeting and anxious to prompt. The Inspector, in a blue serge lounge suit which doubtless he wore on off-duty Sundays, had the repressed and slightly restless manner of one unused to the interiors of places of worship.

"Now, sir," he said, "I'd like your story from beginning to end. I understand that you've found a body. I'd like you to tell me everything you know. Wait a moment and let me explain. I want you to tell me as clearly as possible everything that you've noticed out of the ordinary since you've been with Dr. Garrow."

Roger lowered his gaze and frowned.

"I do not see the least sense in that," he said, "for you would not believe me. I can tell you where to find a body buried in lime; but I can almost promise you that you won't find it if you trouble about the formality of getting a search warrant."

"Why not?"

"Because Dr. Garrow will know, and by the time you get there the body will be gone. Don't ask me how he'll know, but take my word for it that he *will.*"

The Inspector did not demur.

"In the circumstances," he said, "we can manage without a warrant. 'Acting on information received.' It isn't like entering a private residence. Now, sir, I understand there's more than one summerhouse. Could you just draw a rough sketch-map of the grounds, indicating the spot you mean?"

"Yes, I could do that."

"Thank you. That will do presently. And now, Mr. Moorlock, will you kindly go ahead and don't think I shall be doubting you. I know that something right outside the ordinary is going on here, and I've learned a few things about Dr. Garrow before he came to these parts: And because I'm a police officer it doesn't mean that I don't believe in queer things.

"I'll tell you a little story. Before I came to these parts, when I was on another division, two of our men went in plain clothes to catch out a fortune-teller and clairvoyant. She took their money and, after some palaver, told them they were going to be unlucky.

'You've come, here to catch me out,' she said, 'and the unsupported evidence of one of you won't be worth much. For the other—and I won't say which—is going to be knocked down by a car tonight and killed.' And— well, it turned out just as she said. So after that she was let alone. The law doesn't take much count of such things, but the police can believe what they like. We're not discouraged from believing in the Bible. Far from it. And it's in there pretty plain that the Powers of Evil *can* be invoked."

That speech gave Roger just the encouragement that he needed. He began his story and told it to the end without much hesitation. Only once did he falter and that was when he told of the midnight incident in the library and the broom falling from invisible hands.

"Of course you think I dreamed that," he interpolated. "I've got an open mind," Stillby rejoined. "Trode can't keep that great house in order by himself, and there's no other registered servant there. What's more, inquiries have shown quite conclusively that Dr. Garrow never had any other servant in that house. Now don't start getting fidgety again, Mr. Moorlock, and think I'm not believing you. It wouldn't be worth my while to waste time in listening to lies. And besides, don't forget, I'm taking the precaution of listening to you in a church. I wouldn't go that far—would I?—if I thought there was nothing in what you're telling me."

Roger proceeded, still unhappy in his tale, but slightly comforted. He reached the end and after a moment's silence the Inspector spoke again.

"You see, Mr. Moorlock, we're not concerned with whether Dr. Garrow is in league with Old Nick, or thinks he is. All we're concerned with is whether he has committed crime; and, if he has, the end he had in view is no affair of ours.

"Now I am going to take your advice. There is never any harm in being on the safe side. I shall take a man with me tonight and we shall open up the floor of the summerhouse—without a warrant and without so much as By your Leave. If we find a body there, as you describe, we shall proceed to the house and arrest Dr. Garrow and the man Trode on suspicion—"

Roger interrupted.

"Then for God's sake come armed. Are you allowed to, by the way?"

The Inspector looked down his nose.

"Don't worry about that, sir. Regulations are all very well in their way. And coming to that, we're not allowed to take up the floor of his summerhouse without going to him first and stating a reason. But this is an exceptional case—and thank the Lord that it *is* exceptional!" He made the last remark with a wry smile which found a reflection in Roger's face."
"What time will you be coming?" Roger asked.

"Some time in the early morning—between one and three, I expect. I recommend you, sir, not to go to bed. You may be needed."

"All right. I'll come down directly I hear anything. I hope to God you'll get it all over tonight. I'm feeling rotten."

The Inspector nodded sympathetically.

"Yes—and looking it. And I don't wonder. A lot of men who've been through what you have would be crazy by now."

The Vicar interrupted.

"Need he go back, Inspector? Roger, come and stay with us for the night."

"No," said Roger, "I'll be in at the death."

Stillby glanced at the Vicar over his shoulder.

"I'd rather he went back to Dr. Garrow's, sir. You see, he didn't, the Doctor might get suspicious. Besides, we don't quite know what we're up against and we may want help—if this gentleman doesn't mind lending it. And he looks as if he could be useful."

Vallence said nothing for the moment, but spoke again after a pause.

"Very well. Is that all, then?" '

"Yes, sir, thank you. I think that's about all. Except, of course, you won't breathe a word of this to a soul?" The required assurance was given and the Inspector stood up.

"Thank both of you gentlemen very much," he said. "I'll be going now. Or rather I think it might be as well, bearing in mind what Mr. Moorlock says and leaving nothing to chance, if you two gentlemen went out together and left me here for a bit. I can be looking at the hymn books and one thing and another. That's in case anybody should be watching outside. You know what I mean."

"I think you're right," said Roger cordially. "We shall meet—er—at Phillippi, then."

They went out. Roger, following the Vicar, glanced back in the act of closing the door behind him. It was only a glance, but he thought that he saw the Inspector begin to lean forward in the pew.

Outside, Roger missed a step and Vallence's arm came up beneath his- own.

"Here, steady!" said & voice in his ear.

Roger clung to the arm.

"Sorry," he said, "but I reel rotten. He believes it. That's the awful part. He believes it!" Vallence forced a smile in spite of himself.

"Come! Be reasonable. Wouldn't you have been furious if he'd called you a liar?"

"Yes—but I should have been comforted."

Vallence looked at him and partly understood. It was as if he saw the spirit of the Child—which never quite forsakes the Man, no matter how long he lives—peeping out of the strong man's eyes.

"Come along," he said gently, "come along and see Marjory. She'll—well, you won't tell her, of course—but all the same she can help you more than I can. And, if you don't feel up to it tonight, think again and come and stay with us."

"Yes," Roger returned bitterly. "Sick Parade on the eve of battle. Not me!"

"All right. Well try not to worry. You've been through much more than you know. The strain of those weeks in that unearthly atmosphere, and then that vile discovery of last night. Yes, I can understand. But just . think that by tomorrow—humanly speaking—it will all be ended."

"I'm not afraid of two old men," said Roger sullenly. Vallence steadied his arm again.

"I know that," he said. "I know of whom you're afraid. 'And we're taught to fear him—yet not to fear him. Paradoxical that. Well, you've nothing to fear if —but I won't preach to you now. Go and talk to your Marjory. I know she feels that there's something wrong and she wants to comfort you."

She was alone in the drawing-room when he went to her. She looked up at him with a smile; but he suspected that it was the kind of smile one takes to a sick patient's bedside.

"Well, old Fiddle Face?" she said.

"Is it as long as that? Show me how you clasp a fiddle, dear."

"I can't. You're much too big. You're a violin cello. But sit down beside me and put your Fiddle Face on my shoulder. There—poor old lump of worry! Feeling better?"

"Lots better."

He lifted his face a little to look at her; and asked the old question which begs—and generally receives—only one answer.

"Do you still love me?"

"Of course," she whispered.

"Then I don't, care."

"What!" said Marjory laughing, a little lift in her voice.

"I mean—I don't care—about anything else."

CHAPTER XXVI
THE LOST SOUL

Roger did not enjoy the prospect of meeting Dr. Garrow that evening.' It was' not merely because of Garrow's powers of intuition, and. it was not that his own conscience accused him. His conviction that he was acting for the common weal remained as strong as ever. His feelings were analogous to those of the hypersensitive man who will' not willingly see living the creature which is about to be slain for him to eat.

He was waiting in the hall for Trode to give the signal for dinner when Dr. Garrow came downstairs. He had his back to the stairs and Garrow came silently. Roger was unaware of his presence until a white hand dropped on his shoulder. He started violently and exclaimed aloud

"Why now," said Garrow, with only the ghost of a smile, "is that what the lay doctors would call Nerves, or what the pietists would call a Guilty Conscience? Any man with a conscience must necessarily have a guilty one, and neurasthenia is the heirloom of the last noisy and hurried generations. In either case, forgive me." Roger said nothing, but tried to force a smile, Trode appeared and moved towards the gong.

"Since your nerves are deranged," Garrow continued, "We will spare the gong tonight. It is a superfluous formality, seeing that we are both on the spot. But Trode is a creature of habit."

He made no sound—which would have been superfluous so far as Trode was concerned—but stared at the man's back', as Roger had seen him stare before. Trode hesitated and turned, received a look, and went back to the kitchen.

"How do you do that?" Roger asked. "I've seen you do it before."

"Oh, do you want him back?"

Garrow turned and stared at the door which had just closed upon Trode. It opened again at once and Trode looked back, a question in his eyes. Garrow smiled and shook his head and the door closed again.

"That," said the doctor smiling, "comes of close association and a certain amount of practice. Trode is an easy subject. He lacks—and by compensation he gains. Now let us go in to dinner."

It seemed to Roger that Garrow's manner, always laboured, was more portentous than usual. It was as if consciously he walked in the shades of some imminent climax. He had, as yet said nothing to denote his mood, but there was that in his manner which suggested the dreary fortitude of the condemned epicurean. He sat down wearily opposite Roger and Trode appeared with a tureen of soup.

When the man was gone again Roger looked up and met Garrow's eyes. They were sad, suffering, inscrutable, like the eyes of that dreadful vision in the crystal.

"Tomorrow we may—I say we *may*—enjoy a small celebration."

"Indeed?" said Roger, a little huskily.

"Tomorrow is my birthday I shall not tell you how old I am going to be. We had a little jqke once before about my age—if you remember. Well, as regards that I shall not tell you the truth. I am older than I look. But if I live through tomorrow I know that I shall be safe for another year."

"Yes?" said Roger. "Well, that's more than most men would dare to say. And that's also, of course, another little joke."

Garrow laughed softly.

"Oh, no, it isn't. The Ides of March were no joke to Caesar. How do I know—concerning myself? I know a little of astrology, but I confess only a little. Astrology as an exact science died with the Magi. The stars have no clear voice for any man to-day. They give only the least hints of hope and warning—little whispers almost lost to us in the void. Much forbidden knowledge remains for' those who dare to seek it, much more has sunk beneath the tide of time."

He paused and laughed.

"But one mustn't get—what is the modern word for prosy? Anyhow, tell me what you have been doing with yourself to-day in your leisure time. No doubt you have visited a certain lady?"

"Yes," said Roger, gruff with embarrassment. "As you know, she hasn't been too well, but she's a lot better."

"I'll warrant she didn't take the same treatment as yourself. The glass of whisky which I gave you—it did you good, I hope?"

Roger, hot under the watching eye, managed to prevaricate.

"It certainly didn't do me any harm, thank you," he said as lightly as he could. But the while his thoughts were whispering: "He knows! Damn him, I believe he knows! At least he knows that I didn't swallow the stuff."

There was a spell of silence. Roger, looking up, bestowed on Garrow a glance which he had meant to be quick and covert; but his gaze was caught and held. Garrow was quietly regarding him With an air of melancholy severity, and for the moment Roger felt absurdly like a little boy detected by his father in the act of lying. The elder did not speak for a long minute, and when he did he called Roger by his Christian name, as occasionally he had come to do of late.

"I wonder," he said suddenly, "why you do not like me, Roger."

"I haven't said that I didn't."

"Of course not. That would have been rude. And you have done your work—such little work as I have given you to do—quite faithfully and well. Still you are a disappointment. I had once hoped that you were a man with whom I could share a secret. I make few mistakes, but I have made one in you. It is not your fault."

"I am sorry," said Roger simply. He looked straight across at Garrow. "Excuse me," he continued, "but I should like to know exactly what that means. Are you giving me a hint to resign? Or are you preparing me to hear my dismissal?"

Garrow frowned and did not answer immediately.

"I may not need you after tomorrow," he said. "If I find that I do, I shall ask you to stay with me for the customary month. But in any event I shall not send you empty away. I shall add to my cheque' something by way of a wedding present—if I may anticipate the wedding so soon."

Roger looked up, irritated, and embarrassed.

"Excuse me," he said, "but—frankly—I don't want it. I apologise if that sounds rude, but it cannot be helped. I made a bargain with you and I want no more than my dues. The work-»you have set me to do—"

"Is not yet quite finished," said Garrow simply. "You didn't know, and you don't know now what may be going to happen."

"What may be going to happen?" Roger repeated.

"I don't know. And if I did I could not tell you. There -—you are making me talk like a child, and you are getting nothing out of me.[1] It was disastrous that you should know the Vallences. If it were not for that influence I might have had you a very different man."

Roger sat still and frowning..

"What does that mean?" he asked.

"It means that you cannot serve me unless you march under the same banner. But you and I—well, we have not the same allegiance."

It was all clear between them now save for the thinnest of veils. Roger looked squarely across at him. "Thank God!" he said simply.

Garrow started a little and shuddered.

"Not that word, if you please—in this house."

There was complete silence in the room save for a great moth fluttering and striving in a candle shade. Roger would have gone at once, but he had his own reasons for staying one more night. After a minute he heard himself speak in a voice subdued and level and dull. "Yes. I understand. But I didn't want to believe it. I wouldn't quite believe it—until the' last few days. I mustn't judge you. I mustn't sit at your table and tell you what I think of you. But I go tomorrow."

Trode came in and removed the two plates. Garrow took ho notice of him and spoke again. "Very well, Roger. Have it your own way. Go tomorrow if you will. In any event I may not want you ' after tomorrow, and if I do I must go wanting. But I may need you tonight. You have sold me your sword, remember. I may not need it, but—"

"Against what enemy?" Roger interrupted.

Garrow smiled faintly.

"That need not. concern your conscience," he said. "Against nobody and nothing that you would call Good." Roger sat quietly and watched him. There was a ringing in his ears as if a sense of climax were making itself audible.

"Why do you think," he asked in a low voice, "that you may need my help tonight?"

Garrow looked straight back at him for a moment and then lowered his gaze.

"Well, now," he said, "how shall I answer that? You are a very literal young man. If I knew you better and had the right to say it, I might call you painfully literal. How does one know what may happen tonight, or any night? As we sit talking a great many things—totally' unexpected things—are happening in the world. Somewhere in this world—this country, I should say—men are returning home from work, and one finds that his wife has decamped with his neighbour, another that his son is in hospital with a broken limb, another that his daughter has confessed to a fatal indiscretion, and yet another that his mother has been taken suddenly sick and died. We do not know what awaits us around the corner of another hour."

Roger turned over that last phrase, sifting it in his mind before replying.

"Generally speaking we don't," he agreed, "but I thought you did. I haven't forgotten that incident, you know—about the railway accident."

Garrow's slow smile was equivocal with vanity and fear.

"Oh, that? But, my good sir, that was nothing. The science I use is not an exact one. I mean that it is not entirely to be trusted. Tonight is a vastly important night in my life. I am being warned. The Voice is audible, but not coherent. But there is no turning back."

Roger said nothing and to his relief Dr. Garrow too fell into silence. The silent Trode came in and chagged the plates. This evening his face was whiter than ever. Roger caught Garrow in the act of studying the man's face and turned his eyes quickly to see Trode avoiding the gaze. The air which Roger breathed was heavy and charged with electricity as if a storm approached, but beyond the windows the waning daylight lit a placid evening sky.

"And now," said Garrow, when the coffee had been served. "We will go into the library, if you will, and have our last game of chess. I call it our last game, for so it must be if you are leaving me tomorrow. I shall miss our games."

Something smote Roger, but it was a shaft of pity and not of conscience.

"You will be getting someone else," he said gently.

"I shall be needing no one else. It may all be well with me, or it may not. But come along. I think that I can beat you."

"As usual," Roger said, trying to laugh.

They went up to the library and Roger got out the board and set the pieces. He concealed a pawn in either hand and turned to Garrow. Garrow hesitated and touched his left first, and Roger's hand unclosed to show a black piece.

"Very well," said Garrow. "You are white. Turn the board and take the first move."

It seemed to Roger that, although the game was going against himself. Dr. Garrow was not playing so well as usual. Roger had little interest in the game and the end came as a surprise to him. He saw a sudden opportunity to fight back and brought his queen diagonally across the board to remove a pawn and say "Check." Then he leaned back to light a cigarette and wait. After a little while he heard Garrow speak.

"It's mate," he said simply.

"No!" said Roger, laughing and looking at the board. "But it is. Look. I cannot move my king. And how- can I cover him?"

Roger looked and continued to smile.

"Yes," he said, after a few moments, "you are right and I had no idea. I'm sorry because I fluked that. Nobody more surprised than the striker."

Garrow leaned back sighed and passed a hand across his brow. Roger saw the man's eyes and closed his own for an instant before he moved his gaze.

"Ah," said Garrow wearily, "I have tonight something which they call a Blind Spot. That in itself is a warning. 'Clouds, dews and dangers come.' "

He leaned his elbows on the table and pressed his hands to his face. There was a spell of silence before he spoke again.

"I am woefully tired. I wish now I had never seen her."

His voice was dull and distant. Roger was not quite sure if he had been addressed, but politeness urged him to put a question and Garrow answered.

"Oh, she began it—damn her! She came into Tewkesbury two days after the battle—she and her monkey. And she said to me, 'Why now you are a pretty young lording to be wearing the white Yorkshire rose. Come and lie in my lodging tonight and I will make a great lord of thee. And this ape is not what he seems, for he is called Ascaralius and I have suckled him.' "

Something like a cold wind passed through Roger, cutting through the flesh and clinging about his bones.

"What are you saying?" he heard himself ask.

Garrow continued in the same distant voice.

"Poor wench—they burned her in Gloucester town the year following. And Ascaralius they killed with a silverheaded arrow. But the torch had passed to me and I have borne it from that day to this."

The dull voice paused and then presently spoke again. "But there is no going back. It is going forward . . . going on . . . always . . . forever. . ."

He sat on with his hands pressed over his eyes and Roger presently rose.

"You don't want to play anymore?" he asked quietly. "No—I thank you. And you are tired? Well, my dear fellow, go to your room if you will, but do not sleep. For I may need you."

Roger stood, hesitating and uncomfortable.

"But how shall I know?" he asked.

"You will hear. Or Trode shall come. Goodnight, my dear fellow. And tomorrow, when we part, take with you, if you can, a kind thought of me."

Roger afterwards remembered these words, and the infinite weariness and pathos of the voice. For all that he afterwards learned of Garrow it was in his heart to pity him, as indeed he could not help but pity the whole army of the damned.

CHAPTER XXVII
THE ULTIMATE HORROR

Roger sat in his room, smoking and trying to read. He wanted, if possible, to distract his mind, but while his eyes obediently read, the sense of the words remained aloof. He was listening. Hearing dominated and dulled the other senses. The air about him seemed heavy and charged with anticipation. The least noise would have startled him; the silence worried him.

He did not expect the police until the small hours. They would go first to the summer-house and make their discovery. Afterwards he would hear the bell sound below stairs. And then—and then imagination halted at the end of a blind alley.

If Garrow practised the Black Arts—and Roger in the face of all that he would have called sane now believed that he did—there might yet be some way out for him. But Garrow himself seemed to have a presentiment. If there were truth in the things which he had hinted, the reckoning for nearly five-hundred years had fallen due.

The hands of the clock went round, crossing the threshold of midnight, but the house stayed quiet. It was after two before he heard a word. He stood up, frowning and straining his ears. Somewhere below he had heard a soft thud and the gentle closing of a door.

A ringing started in his ears as he stood rigid to listen. Through it he heard—or thought he heard, for he could not be sure—footfalls about the house and muffled voices. But those half-audible sounds died away and left him still unsure if he had heard or imagined them.

The silence lingered on and the time dragged towards a dreadful ultimate moment which brought a shock like the smashing and splintering of glass. Somewhere below a scream rang out, long, dreadful and shrill and infinitely daunting.

Roger started violently, leaped up and ran to his door.. As he opened it the house seemed full of shoutings and running footfalls. After the long silence', sound, released, was running riot.

Roger ran along the landing to the stairhead. Light welled up from the hall below like a luminous mist, and guided him. A throttled scream, more dreadful than the first, rang out from below, and then a voice in mortal agony. The voice was shockingly distorted, but he knew it at once for Garrow's.

"Father of Lies, thou hast betrayed me!"

Sharp upon the words came another frozen and throaty shriek and the crash of a falling body.

As one who runs in a nightmare, Roger ran to the head of the stairs. He reached it just as the door in the outer hall was flung open with a crash, and a cold draught sprang up to meet him. Roger started to run downstairs, but checked himself with a jerk which nearly sent him headlong.

At the bottom of the stairs a body lay huddled. He recognised it at once as Trode's. He climbed down slowly and shudderingly towards it and another body, prostrate in the hall, came into his range of vision. Dr. Garrow lay with his head in a pool of a deeper hue than the purple robe which clothed him from neck to ankle.

Roger, three or four stairs from the bottom, bent over Trode and suddenly sickened and reeled. He clung for a moment to the balustrade to save himself from pitching forward on to that mangled body. He needed but just that one look to be sure that the man was dead. His throat had been torn out as if by the claws of some monstrous beast.

Another cry rang out, and Roger knew that it was himself that uttered it. Clinging to the balustrade and shutting his eyes, he edged his way past the body and ran to the prostrate form of Garrow.

As with Trode, so with Garrow. Roger reeled away' from the sight of the torn throat and the twisted windpipe. He turned towards the open door, crying aloud for help, and began to run and stagger dazedly in curves. He tripped, or slipped on the top step and came heavily down the rest, falling on hands which were scarified and torn by gravel.

"Help!" he shouted; and it seemed to him that he heard an echo. He ran on blindly, continuing to shout, until his shouting changed abruptly to another cry of horror.

As he recoiled and then bent to stare, he heard heavy footfalls running. A voice which he vaguely recognised was calling to him, and he could see dimly the forms of men in uniform approaching at a run.

"All right, sir! Are you all right?"

"Here!" he cried wildly. *"Here!"*

He forced himself to bend over the body. It was that of a tall, elderly, white bearded man. He knew it at once—without ever knowing how he knew—to be that of Professor Thurley. The corpse stolen from its grave had come to light at last.

There was blood on the white hands and in the nails, and little of the look of death about him. The face was plump, the body swollen. And Roger screamed like a trapped hare and stood pointing.

"Look! Look there! He's bloated and glutted with blood!"

A policeman caught him as he sagged, swayed and began to fall. A black, woolly mist rose up before his eyes, enveloping him, shutting out sight and mercifully stealing all consciousness from him.

Roger was gently laid beside the drive and the police hastened on into the house. It was a long while before Roger learned a little of what they found. He never learned all.

CHAPTER XXVIII
FINALE

Mr. Chester, the solicitor, who was also the local coroner, presented himself at the Vicarage at a time when an invitation to tea—and consequently a general talk with all three resident members of the family— seemed more probable than merely possible. For he was a worried, besides being a mystified, man ; and the exigencies of his calling combined, with personal curiosity in urging him to straighten a tangled and very important business.
A maid was carrying tea things through the hall when he mounted the steps, and she laid the tray aside to come and speak to him before tapping at the drawing-room door to announce him. She ushered him inside and went to get another cup and saucer.

Mr. Chester went in, bowed to Mrs. Vallence and Marjory, smiled meaningly at the Vicar and accepted a chair. He inquired after the health of the ladies, rose to take the cup of tea which he saw to be ready, asked Vallence how he did, and was about to proceed when Vallence took advantage of a slight hesitation.

"Now, Chester," he said, smiling, "we know what you want. Roger's taken a turn for the better, I'm glad to say. At least, Davis and Grimshaw both think so."

"Is he—er—compos yet?"

"No, but they say he's coming through. Temporary failure of the nervous system. He's been within a paper's breadth of brain fever. And I—knowing what I do— don't wonder at it. We shan't know what poor Roger's been through until he can tell us."

Chester nodded gravely two or three times.

"That's exactly the point. Nobody wants to worry the poor fellow, but—the Home Office has been badgering me. As you know, I've had to postpone the inquest—*inquests,* I mean—twice. Can't do anything without his evidence. And with the whole country watching and waiting for news—well, it's extremely awkward."

Vallence smiled grimly.

"It's much more awkward than you think. It's, just as well that you'll have to hold those inquests before Roger is fit to get about again, because you wouldn't believe the principal witnesses, if you heard them in court, or if you did they'd say up in Whitehall that you were just as insane as everybody else. And what would be said of the police? *They're* dreading is as much as anybody. *They're* going to be considered mad when everything comes out—if they tell the truth."

Chester set down his cup and saucer.

"You seem to know a great deal," he said. "I wish you'd tell me."

"Officially or unofficially?"

"Unofficially—now."

"All right. I'm not an actual witness, so don't ask me to stand up and repeat what I'm going to tell you with a Testament in my hand. I shall jib at that—and so will everybody else who has any knowledge of this ghastly business. Anyhow, as I've said, you wouldn't dare accept the evidence you'd be getting. Now cast your mind back a very short while. What began the troubles about here?"

Chester shrugged his shoulders.

"The desecration of the grave and the theft of old Thurley's body."

"Just so—And then the murder of my man Smith. The two were not unconnected. Smith helped to steal the body, went on the drink with the money he got and became dangerous because of his tongue. So Garrow— who had employed him—deputed that monster Trode to kill him; and at the same time arranged quite a plausible alibi for Trode. He got Roger to hear him talking to Trode, when Trode was actually out of the house and doing his killing.

"And now I suppose you want to know where all this comes from and whither it leads. Garrow was a Satanist. Heaven only knows how old the man really was, and what were his antecedents, but he'd kept himself alive by—yes, infernal means. Father Rowlinson gave me a hint or two about him, and another hint or two about the whole, unspeakable business. "Thurley died with a valuable secret—or Garrow thought he did. Garrow stole the body in order to infuse life into it for a short while by—yes, Black Magic—in order to extract that secret . .'. er—by torture if necessary. I don't know the ghastly *modus operandi* of bringing temporary life to a dead body, but I have been told that it entails *the blood and the breath of the dying*.. Hence the disappearance of tramps—about whom nobody is likely to inquire too urgently. Garrow and Trode bungled it several times. That is why the remains of five tramps have so far come to light.

"When at last they were successful you see now what happened. It was not Thurley's own gentle spirit which returned for a very brief space to its old abode; it was a demon which turned on those who had conjured it and rent out their throats like a wild beast. Poor Roger ran down into it all just after Thurley had—I mean just after he had been dispossessed. The poor fellow had been warned of the kind of house he was living in and he'd already had enough experience to convince him that things were very .wrong indeed. That night was the last straw. I wonder he isn't going to be permanently insane—but they say he won't be." Vallenoe paused and cleared his throat.

"Poor chap, he's had a rough time in more ways than one. But I've got a job for him at a good school—as soon as he's fit to take it. Well, I think that's about all I can tell you, although I'm prepared to answer any questions if I can."

Chester had been sitting quite still. Then, without taking his gaze off the Vicar, he fumbled for his handkerchief and blew violently through his nose.

"If," he said with a short gasp, "that is the sort of story you think I can allow to be told in my Court—" Words failed him and he came to a sudden stop.

"I don't," said Vallence simply. "Even if the truth came out and one or two believed it, I don't see that it could be for the common good. You'd better go to the police and all lay your heads together and concoct something first. Garrow was a homicidal maniac. On that awful night one of then—Garrow or Trode or the decoyed tramp—went Bersac, killed the other two and then committed suicide. It's not very good, but it—or something like it will have to do. Write to the Home Office and get them to request the Press not to be too inquisitive—the sort of news unsuitable for public consumption. That's what I would suggest."

Chester bowed his head and began to rub his forehead. "I never dreamed—I never dreamed of being placed in such a position," he said huskily.

Mrs. Vallence answered him and by contrast her tone was very dry.

"Nor did anybody else who has had anything at all to do with this dreadful affair. I'm sure—"

She was interrupted. The door sprang open and a nurse appeared. She was full of unprofessional excitement.

"He's come round!" she exclaimed. "Just as Doctor said he would."

Marjory and her Father both sprang up.

"He woke up after a good sleep and looked at me and wanted to know where he was. So I told him and then—"

"I'll go to him at once," said Vallence, taking a" step towards the door.

"I beg your pardon/Vicar, but—" the nurse hesitated and smiled, "—it was Miss Marjory he asked for."

"Oh?" said the Vicar, faltering. "Oh—er—well—"

But Marjory was already half way across the room— and talking.

"All right, Nurse. I know exactly, what to do. I mustn't let him get excited, and I mustn't stay with him too long, and I've got to promise to come and see him again very soon, and—well, you lead the way and tell him I'm coming."

A minute later she was kneeling beside the bed. "Hullo, Roger, darling."

"Hullo, darling. How are you? I say, I've been ill, haven't I?"'

"Yes, but you're lots better now."

"I know'. But I've been having bad dreams—terrible dreams. About a man named Garrow. Garrow, now? Was there ever such a man as Garrow?"

"Hush! Never mind about that. Try to forget."

"Yes. But I don't see how I can ever—Yet I don't know. I think I'm beginning to forget a little already— with my head on your shoulder."

"There will always be my shoulder for you to rest on," said Marjory softly.

A.M. Burrage – The Life And Times.

Alfred McLelland Burrage, better known as simply AM Burrage, was born in Hillingdon, Middlesex on July 1st, 1889, to Alfred Sherrington Burrage and Mary E. Burrage. On his Father's side writing already ran in the family's blood as both he and an uncle, Edwin Harcourt Burrage, were writers of the then very popular boys' magazine fiction.

Life in late Victorian times was by no means easy and writing has always been a precarious career for most. For an insight into the young AM and his surroundings it is interesting to see how certain facts were captured in the 1891 census when he was aged one. The family is listed as living at Uxbridge Common in Hillingdon. His father is 40 and his mother 36. In the next census of 1901, and with it the end of the Victorian era, the family has moved to 1 Park Villa, Newbury. In that time his father has aged 17 years his mother 6 years and young AM has disappeared from the records. It's almost a precursor to one of his stories.

There is little documented about his growing up and education. What we can glean though is something about his environment. His neighbours were varied: a tailor's journeyman, a corn porter, a lodging-house keeper and a grocer's assistant. Nothing particularly illustrious, so times cannot have been as rosy as they should, especially in the light of his Father's hard work. Alfred Sherrington wrote for The Boy's World, Our Boys' Paper, The Boys of England, and various others. He also appears to have written under the pseudonym Philander Jackson and edited The Boys' Standard and that one of his more celebrated pieces was a retelling of the story of Sweeney Todd entitled "The String of Peals; or, Passages from the Life of Sweeney Todd, the Demon Barber".

Sadly Alfred Sherrington Burrage died in 1906. There is a biographical note in Lloyd's Magazine, from 1921, which suggests that young Alfred McLelland was studying at St. Augustine's, the Catholic Foundation School in Ramsgate, and most probably away from home at the time.

A.M. Burrage was 16 years old when he had his first story published; the same year as his father's death, in the prestigious boys' paper, Chums. It was a great start to his professional career and whether doors had been opened by his father and family or not the young man's career now had to stand on its own. He was now primary provider for the household and this was the only way he could do it. His Mother, sister and aunt must be provided for.

Magazine fiction was his family's blood and business and for A. M. Burrage, business was good. He established himself as a competent and creative writer and was busy writing stories and articles on a weekly basis for publications such as Boys' Friend Weekly, Boys' Herald, Comic Life, Vanguard, Dreadnought, Triumph Library Cheer Boys Cheer, and Gem, under the pseudonym 'Cooee'.

However, unlike his father and uncle who had remained firmly and easily categorised as boys' writers, he had his sights set on the more well regarded, more lucrative, adult market. Burrage was aided in his early years as a professional writer by Isobel Thorne of the off-Fleet Street publishing firm Shurey's. Her publications have been characterised as "low in price, modest in payments, but whose readers were avid for romance, thrills, sensation, strong characterisation and neat plotting", and this estimation of her publications also fits nicely the description of Burrage's own writing at that time. For a young writer this sort of readership was vital, and the modest wages he received were bolstered by the exposure the publications brought him. Burrage was certainly helped by Thorne's use of young writers.

At the time Burrage was beginning to really establish himself as a writer, the entire magazine fiction scene was benefiting from what we would now see as disruptive influences: new printing techniques, a growing readership with more disposable income and leisure time and other media failing to provide – though obviously movies and such were only in their infancy at the time. The market was lively and commercial, and the readership interested, excitable and willing to pay. P. G. Wodehouse, of Jeeves fame, recalls these years:

We might get turned down by the Strand, but there was always the hope of landing with Nash's, the Story-teller, the London, the Royal, the Red, the Yellow, Cassell's, the New, the Novel, the Grand, the Pall Mall, and the Windsor, not to mention Blackwood's, Cornhill, Chambers's and probably about a dozen more I've forgotten.

With War clouds darkening the skies of Europe in 1914 Burrage was firmly established as a magazine writer, securing publication in London Magazine and The Storyteller, which were both highly prestigious publications. Alongside he had plenty printed in less illustrious publications such as Short Stories Illustrated.

By now Burrage, a young man of twenty-four-year-was eligible for the Armed Services. Under the 'Derby Scheme' he confirmed that he was available for service if called upon in December 1915. Conscription was to follow shortly though, by that time, Burrage had already voluntarily enrolled in the Artists Rifles.

The significance of Burrage's decision to join the Artists Rifles is made clear by the nature of the unit itself. They formed in the middle of the nineteenth century, a group of volunteer artists comprising musicians, writers, painters and engravers. Minerva and Mars were their patrons, one of wisdom, arts, and defence, the other of war. The unit boasted several significant figures as ex-servicemen, including Dante Gabriel Rossetti, Algernon Charles Swinburne and William Morris. It was a popular unit with students and recent postgraduates, and the training was considered and extensive.

In Burrage's vivid, celebrated account of World War I entitled War is War, he insists that he was a volunteer and not a conscript, though as has already been noted, it is quite possible that his decision to join such a respected territorial unit may have been more of an effort to secure himself a more congenial army posting; had he waited for conscription, he would have had little choice over those with whom he was posted. Unlike poets Wilfred Owen or Edward Thomas, Burrage did not achieve a commission, and he suggests in War is War that this may be a result of his extremely unmilitary personality and his shortcomings as a soldier.

Add to this the fact that as the breadwinner for the family he was putting himself in harm's way. If anything were to happen to him the result on the family would be devastating. With the death of
Edwin Harcourt Burrage in 1916 it came even more starkly into focus.

Even though he was now a soldier he was still a writer and writers had to write. It also helped that it was a distraction from the mindless carnage around him. He experimented with various genres, excelling in the one that was to prove most lucrative for him; the light romance, in which a male character invariably meets a female character, there is a problem or hurdle to their being together, they overcome it and they live happily ever after. Burrage's talent for this formula was such that he could work seemingly endless minor variations from the same basic storyline and so he was able to keep writing a steady body of easy work.

He gives a fascinating account of the practicalities of writing such fiction during wartime in War is War, in which he remarks on the difficulties of censorship: "the problem of censorship was an acute one to me. It was well enough to write a story, but the difficulty was to get it censored. Officers were shy of tackling five thousand words or so, written in indelible pencil..." After some time he managed to find a chaplain who was willing to undertake the censorship. However, in order to secure this chaplain's favour and thus his services he was obliged to appear to be holy. Though he did so in earnest while he was with the chaplain, his efforts were dashed when the chaplain found him, sprawled on top of a young girl, and realised Burrage's piety to be a fraudulent con. As Burrage had anticipated, the reality of his behaviour ensured that this particular opportunity was swiftly ended. Resourceful to the last, though, he writes of his solution: "there were 'green envelopes' which could be sent away sealed and were liable only to censorship at the base, but these were only sparingly issued... I met an A.S.C. lorry driver who had stolen enough green envelopes to last me for the rest of the war; and since he only wanted two francs for them I was free of the censorship from that day forward."

Although we know that Burrage had his family to support at home as an incentive to keep writing, at times in War is War he reveals a more intimate aspect of his relationship with his work.

"It was a great relief to me to write when it was at all possible – to sit down and lose myself in that pleasant old world I used to know and pretend to myself that there never had been a war. Some of my editors seemed of the opinion that we were not suffering from one now. One used to write to me saying "Couldn't you let me have one of your light, charming love stories of country house life by next Thursday." I would get these letters in the trenches during the usual 'morning hate' when my fingers were too numb to hold a pencil, when I was worn out with work and sleeplessness, and when I was extremely doubtful if there ever would be another Thursday".

Writing is a useful therapy and for Burrage it provided a means to escape if only for a short time to a world that he could control and move at will. With the misery and harsh conditions of the War dragging on he was eventually invalided and so he returned to England.

One of the best insights we have as to the character which Burrage presented on his return from the war is to be found in Lloyd's's 1920 publication of Captain Dorry, one of Burrage's story series. In that publication there was included a brief sketch of Burrage, describing his personality.

A.M. BURRAGE is the type of young man who might very well walk out of one of his own stories. He commenced yarn-spinning as a boy of fifteen at St Augustine's, Ramsgate, writing stories of school life to provide himself with pocket-money. Since then he has won his spurs as one of the most popular of magazine writers. Everything he does has charm and reflects his own romantic spirit – for he is incurably romantic and hopelessly lazy. It is his misfortune, although he would not admit it, that his work finds a too ready market. Nevertheless, his friends hope that one day he will wake up and do justice to himself. Otherwise he may end up as a "best-seller", a fate which doubtless he contemplates with equanimity.

Despite the sketch's fairly accurate but negative summation of Burrage's literary output up to that point, some of his stories seem to exhibit a desire to write about more than just his usual romantic plots. The most immediate change of this nature is in his decision to bring some of his wartime experience into his work, despite being perfectly aware that such writing was not at all what his editors desired, for they feared it would upset and intimidate their readership.

An example of this can be found in "A Town of Memories", published in 1919 in Grand Magazine, in which he uses his well rehearsed romantic story with a slight shift of emphasis to explore his own return from the war and the general reception which soldiers received on their return. Following a young officer as he returns to the town in which he grew up, Burrage portrays an almost hostile environment into which he returns; he is unrecognised, and nobody pays any interest, respect or attention to him or his stories of the war, nor even to his reception of the Distinguished Service Order. Instead, the people of the town have their own interests and priorities with which to concern themselves. Though this contentious portrayal of post-war society certainly marks a slight shift in Burrage's writing, he returns to the romantic convention expected of him by reuniting the officer with a beautiful girl who had admired him throughout school. It would be harsh to not accept that market conditions expected one thing and to ignore them would mean turning his back on publications who still clamoured for his penmanship.

Another of Burrage's alternative directions is to be found in "The Recurring Tragedy", in which a General whose war tactics of attrition had been to the slaughtered cost of his soldiers, and he comes to re-imagine his own past as a Judas figure in a terrible vision. The Strange Career of Captain Dorry became a series for Lloyd's Magazine in 1920 about a gentleman crook and an ex-officer with a Military Cross who, idle in peacetime, meets a mysterious man called Fewgin whose business is in stolen goods and mind reading. Fewgin realises Dorry is a suitable candidate for recruitment into his gang of like-minded ex-military thieves, stealing only from "certain vampires who made money out of the war, and, by keeping up prices, are continuing to make money out of the peace". Again, in this motive, we see a glimpse of Burrage's own feelings on the war, as there is undoubtedly a bitterness towards those profiting from the suffering of others in such a manner. Fewgin justifies himself, saying:

"I help brave men who cannot help themselves. I give them a chance to get back a little of their own from the men who battened and fattened on them, who helped to starve their dependents while they were fighting, who smoked fat cigars in the haunts of their betters, and hoped the war might never end."

Burrage began to see slightly more success in the 1920s, achieving a couple of hard back publications entitled Some Ghost Stories and Poor Dear Esme. The latter, a comedy, concerns a boy who, for various reasons, is forced to disguise himself as a girl. Though these hard cover publications were a notable achievement, and one of which he was proud, the fact was that there was less money in it than in the magazines. In his history of the Strand Magazine, Reginald Pound portrays Burrage around this time, likening him to his equally prolific contemporary Herbert Shaw, considering them "two Bohemian temperaments that suffused and at times confused gifts from which more was expected than come forth. They had a precise knowledge of the popular short story as the product of calculated design. Both privately despised it, though it was their living."

The early 1920s, and with them a boom in prosperity, hope and happiness, now brought with them an increase in demand for war stories. Rather than preferring to ignore the atrocities of the war, which had seemed the general attitude in the immediate post-war years, society became more interested and concerned with the manner in which the war was fought, and the greed and political battles which had necessitated such bloodshed. Burrage answered this demand in 1930 with his own epochal piece, War Is War. He published under the pseudonym 'Ex-Private X', saying "were it otherwise I could not tell the truth about myself", though its publisher, Victor Gollancz, "who published the book and greatly admired it, had to point out that the critics would hardly take the book seriously if it became known that the author earned his living producing two or three slushy love stories a week".

In one of a series of letters he wrote to his contemporary and fellow writer Dorothy Sayers, Burrage bemoans how War is War "promised to be a great success, but was only a moderate one". The book itself was received with reviews on both sides of the spectrum. Cyril Fall's War Books, a survey of post-war writing published in 1930, gives a clear indication as to why the critics were so mixed in reception of the book. He writes:

This book is extremely uneven in quality. The account of the attack at Paschendaele and of conditions at Cambrai after the great German counter-attack are very good indeed; in fact among the best of their kind. But the rest is disfigured by an unreasoned and unpleasant attack on superiors and all troops other than those of the front line, which is all the more astonishing because the author is inclined to harp upon his social position as compared with that of many of the officers with whom he came in contact. He does not use as much bad language as many writers on the War, but his methods of abuse will leave on some of his readers at least a worse impression than the most highly-spiced language.

Dorothy Sayers was the editor at Victor Gollanz for anthologies of ghost and horror stories which included stories by Burrage. She says, in one of her letters of Burrage's story The Waxwork, a piece beyond the nerves of the editors, "what you say about "The Waxwork" sounds very exciting, just the sort of thing I want. Our nerves are stronger than those of the editors of periodicals, and we will publish anything, so long as it does not bring us into conflict with the Home Secretary". Though their correspondence began as strictly business,

Burrage's acquaintance with Atherton Fleming, Sayers's husband, allowed their interactions to become less formal and friendlier. Burrage wrote of Fleming "I hope to encounter him soon in one of the Fleet Street tea-shops". 'Tea-shop' being a popular euphemism for the pub, where both Burrage and Fleming could frequently be found, though their alcohol consumption came to damage both their health and their professions, with Burrage coming off the worse.

Happily for Burrage, as a result of being featured in one of Sayers's anthologies, The Waxwork became one of his best-known stories and it would grab the attention of the film companies several times down the years even becoming an episode in the TV series 'Alfred Hitchcock Presents'.

The developing friendship between Burrage and Sayers enabled him to reveal more details of his personal life, admitting to her his "neuritis at both ends (legs and eyes)", and hinting at his troubles with alcohol: "Fleet Street is not a good place for a man who delights in succumbing to temptation, and whose doctor says that even small doses of alcohol are poison to him". Sayers sympathises, replying that Fleming "agrees with you entirely about the temptations of Fleet Street; he has, however, succeeded, through sheer strength of character, in being able to drink soda-water in the face of all his fellow journalists".

In another of Burrage's letters, he apologises for a delay in sending proofs of a story, with the words:

I have had a pretty thin time lately through illness and anxiety. And for days on end haven't had the energy in me to write a letter, and when I had the energy to send a complete set of proofs to you I found I hadn't the postage money (This is when you take out your handkerchief and start sobbing). I owed my late agent over £1000, so I got practically nothing out of War is War. He stuck to it. Well, he is paid off now, and so are my arrears of income tax. All this took a toll of my very small earning capacity, and I have been sold up. This on top of something which promised to be a great success and was only a moderate one, was a bit too much for me. Still, in spite of sickness I am resilient and shall float again. "You can't keep a good man down," as the whale said about Jonah.

For a man who had so many stories in so many magazines, and was gaining pace in Sayers's anthologies as a talented writer of horror stories, his income will have been far higher than the then average wage, and yet as he says, he finds himself short of money.

Several questions are left unanswered about his personal life. It is unclear whether he was still supporting family, or whether he spent the majority of his money on alcohol, or whether he chose to conceal his true fortunes from those around him. Perhaps most incongruous is the apparent absence of a wife; though his death certificate indicates that he had one, listed as H.A. Burrage, he seems never to mention her to Sayers.

He was around forty-two when he wrote that apology letter to Sayers, though in tone and circumstance it seems to be from a man in a far later stage of his life.

Burrage continued writing until his death in 1956, and continued to be prolifically published. Indeed, the Evening News alone published some forty of his stories between 1950-56. His death is recorded at Edgware General Hospital on 18th December, and the causes of his death are recorded as congestive cardiac failure, arteriosclerosis and chronic bronchitis. He was sixty-seven years old, and his last address is listed as 105 Vaughan Road, Harrow.

Though his name is not often remembered in lists of prominent writers of his time, or even it's genres, his ghost stories are highly regarded by critics and fans alike, while his life story tells us much about the trials and stresses placed on authors during and after the war, and on soldiers returning from that war. His reluctant acceptance that the money was in the magazines while the esteem was in the poorly-paying hard covers, and his persistence as a writer, speak of a determined man, doomed to circumstance yet living as best he could.

In ending A.M Burrage wrote a few sentences which best sum up two things. Firstly his love for his son Simon (who sadly passed away in October 2013 and was a great and passionate advocate for his Father's works.) and secondly his succinct reasons for writing.

TO JULIAN SIMON FIELD BURRAGE
who at the moment of writing will
soon achieve the great age of four.
From somebody who loves him.

In War is War I admitted being a professional writer, or in other words one who depends for his bread and cheese and beer on writing, typing or dictating strings of sentences which his masters, the Public, are kind enough to buy and presumably to read.

The book brought me letters from a few old friends and a great many new ones. A large percentage of the new friends, who missed having seen that my identity was rather unkindly betrayed by the Press, wrote and asked (a) who I was and (b) what sort of stories did I write?

The answer to the second question will be found in the following pages. The answer to the first question is 'Nobody Much', worse luck.

Most of these stories were written with the intention of giving the reader a pleasant shudder, in the hope that he will take a lighted candle to bed with him—for candle-makers must be considered in these hard times. Some have already made their bow from the pages of the monthly magazines. The best have, quite naturally, been rejected.